Faulkner's Folly

By Carolyn Wells

Originally published in 1917

Faulkner's Folly

© 2011 Resurrected Press
www.ResurrectedPress.com

Published by Resurrected Press

This classic book was handcrafted by Resurrected Press. Resurrected Press is dedicated to bringing high quality classic books back to the readers who enjoy them. These are not scanned versions of the originals, but, rather, quality checked and edited books meant to be enjoyed!

Please visit ResurrectedPress.com to view our entire catalogue!

ISBN 13: 978-1-937022-36-5

Printed in the United States of America

FOREWORD

Faulkner's Folly is a classic Carolyn Wells mystery. There is the impossible crime—the murder of a wealthy artist, alone in his studio—to which no one could obtain access without being seen. There is the setting—an elaborate mansion with curious architectural features. There is a hint of the supernatural. Finally, there is one of Wells' detectives—wise men who can see what others do not.

Carolyn Wells' mysteries are more than just detective stories, they are tales of manners of a bygone age, a time when people, of the better sort at least, dressed for dinner, a man never went outside without a hat, and women had a subservient role in society. Not that the author approved of the latter. Many of the murders in her books are of overbearing, abusive or tyrannical husbands, fathers, or lovers, and the prime suspect is often a young defenseless woman who has been taken advantage of or who is being persecuted for trying to assert her independence. Yet marriage is portrayed as the only route to financial security.

In *Faulkner's Folly*, the subject of love and happiness is central. The murder victim is in love with his young model and not his wife. His wife is in love with an old beau. The son is in love with the model. The model, well her affections are uncertain. All this provides grounds not only for suspicions against each of them in turn, but for fears on the part of each that their loved one is actually the murderer. As with all of Wells' books, it is the interaction of the various characters that forms the core of the series, and not crime and detection.

A prominent feature of *Faulkner's Folly* is the supernatural element. The occult, real or fake, plays a role in a number of Wells' mysteries. At the time it was written, the early part of the 20th century, spiritualism, and the belief in paranormal powers such as clairvoyance, were part of the popular culture. Séances, mediums, and ghosts appeared frequently in the literature of the era, and Wells certainly was willing to take advantage of the public interest in the subject by including it as a feature of her novels.

Wells, of course, was famous for her so called "architectural mysteries" in which some architectural element of the house in which the murder takes place plays an important role, and *Faulkner's Folly* is no exception. The murder takes place in the studio of the artist, a repurposed ballroom which can be entered only by three doors, each of which was under close observation at the time of the crime. Almost from the beginning, Wells leaves clues for the reader as to the nature of the secret, but it is not completely revealed until the last chapter.

Surprisingly, for a mystery, detectives play only a minor part in the story. The official police are represented by the unfortunately named "Bobsy" Roberts, a competent but uninspiring policeman who is well meaning but out of his depths. Most of the actual detection is done by the suspects themselves. Only at the end does the true professional detective come in, in this case Alan Ford, and with a few pointed questions and a close surveillance of the crime scene arrive at the solution to the mystery. Not for Wells the charismatic detective such as Hercule Poirot or even Mrs. Marple to come in and take charge, which perhaps explains the fact that Wells' mysteries are not as familiar to modern audiences as Christie's.

Faulkner's Folly is, in many ways, one of Wells' best mysteries. The solution to the crime is not obvious until the end, yet Wells treats the reader fairly by presenting the evidence in an honest manner, and of course, the murderer is the person least suspect. It is with pleasure that Resurrected Press brings you this edition of *Faulkner's Folly*.

About the Author

Carolyn Wells, June 18, 1862 - March 26, 1942 was an American writer and poet. She was best known for her books of poetry and humor until around 1910 she read one of Anna Katherine Green's mysteries and took up the genre. Many of her mysteries featured the detective Fleming Stone. She was married to Hadwin Houghton, heir to the Houghton-Mifflin publishing company. She was a collector of poetry by other authors, and, upon her death, she bequeathed her collection of the works of Walt Witman to the Library of Congress.

Greg Fowlkes
Editor-In-Chief
Resurrected Press
www.ResurrectedPress.com

TABLE OF CONTENTS

CHAPTER 1: IN THE STUDIO

BEATRICE FAULKNER paused a moment, on her way down the great staircase, to gaze curiously at the footman in the lower hall. A perfectly designed and nobly proportioned staircase is perhaps the finest indoor background for a beautiful woman, but though Mrs. Faulkner had often taken advantage of this knowledge, there was no such thought in her mind just now. She descended the few remaining steps, her eyes still fixed on the astonishing sight of a footman's back, when he should have been standing at attention. He might not have heard her soft footfall, but he surely had no business to be peering in at a door very slightly ajar.

Faulkner's Folly was the realised dream of the architect who had been its original owner. It was a perfect example of the type known in England as Georgian and in our own country as Colonial, a style inspired by the Italian disciples of Palladio, and as developed by Inigo Jones and Christopher Wren, it had seemed to James Faulkner to possess the joint qualities of comfort and dignity that made it ideal for a home. The house was enormous, the rooms perfectly proportioned, and the staircase had been the architect's joy and delight. It showed the wooden wainscoting, which had handed down from the Jacobeans; broad, deep steps with low risers, large, square landings, newels with mitred tops and rather plain balusters. But the carved wood necessary to carry out the plans, the great problems of lighting, the necessity for columned galleries and long, arched and recessed windows, together with the stupendous outlay for appropriate grounds and gardens, overtaxed the available funds and Faulkner's Folly, in little more than two years after its completion, was sold for less than its intrinsic value.

James Faulkner died, some said of a broken heart, but his wife had weathered the blow, and was, at the present time, a guest in what had been her own home.

The man who bought Faulkner's Folly was one who could well appreciate all its exquisite beauty and careful workmanship. Eric Stannard, the artist and portrait painter, of international reputation and great wealth, and a friend of long standing, took Faulkner's house with much joy in the acquisition and sympathy for the man who must give it up.

A part of the purchase price was to be a portrait of Mrs. Faulkner by the master hand of the new owner; but Faulkner's death had postponed this, and now, a widow of two years, Beatrice was staying at the Stannards' while the picture was being painted. Partly because of sentiment toward her husband's favourite feature of the house, and partly because of her own recognition of its artistic possibilities, Beatrice had chosen the stairs as her background, and rarely did she descend them without falling into pose for a moment at the spot she had selected for the portrait.

But on this particular evening, Beatrice had no thought of her picture, as she noticed the strange sight of the usually expressionless and imperturbable footman, with his face pressed against the slight opening of the studio door.

"Blake," she said, sharply, and then stopped, regretting her speech. As the Stannards' guest, she had no right or wish to reprove her hosts' servants, but it was well-nigh impossible for her to forget the days of her own rule in that house.

Even as she looked, the man turned toward her a white and startled face,—it seemed almost as if he welcomed her appearance.

"Blake! What is it?" she said, alarmed at his manner. "What are you doing?"

"I—heard a strange sound, Madame,—from the studio—"

"A strange sound?" and Beatrice came along the hall toward the footman.

"And the lights in there, just went out—"

"The lights went out! What do you mean, Blake? It is not your business if lights in rooms are turned off or on, is it?"

"No, Madame—but—there, Madame! Did you not hear that?"

"Oh, yes, yes," and Beatrice paled, as an indistinct voice seemed to cry faintly, "Help!" It was a horrible, gurgling sound, as of one in dire extremity. "What can it be? Go in, Blake, at once! Turn on the lights I—"

"Yes, Madame," and the trembling footman pushed open the door and felt fumblingly in the dark for the electric switch.

It was only a few seconds, but it seemed an interminable time before the lights flashed on and the great room was illuminated to its furthest corners.

Beatrice, close behind the trembling footman, stood, stunned.

"I knew it was something dreadful!" Blake cried, forgetting in his shock his conventional speech.

Beatrice gave one gasping "Oh!" and covered her face with her hands. But in a moment she nerved herself to the sight, and stared, in a horrified fascination, at the awful scene before her.

At the other end of the long room, in a great, carved armchair, sat Eric Stannard, limp and motionless. From his breast protruded an instrument of some sort, and a small scarlet stain showed on the white expanse of his shirt bosom.

"Is he—is he—" began Beatrice, starting

forward to his assistance, when her bewildered eyes took in the rest of the scene.

Behind Stannard, and across the room from one another, were two women. They were Joyce, his wife, and Miss Vernon, a model.

Joyce, only a few feet from her husband's left shoulder, was glaring at Natalie Vernon, with a wild expression of fear and terror, Natalie was huddled against the opposite wall, near the outer door, cowering and trembling, her hands clutching her throat, as if to suppress an involuntary scream.

Unable to take in this startling scene at a glance, Beatrice and Blake stared at the unbelievable tableau before them. The man got his wits together first.

"We must do something," he muttered, starting toward his master. "There is some accident—"

As if by this vitalised into action, the two women behind Stannard came forward, one on either side of him, but only his wife went near to him.

"Eric," she said, faintly, taking his left hand, as it hung at his side. But she got no further. With one glance at his distorted face she sank to the ground almost fainting.

"Who did this, sir?" Blake cried out, standing before Stannard. The dying man attempted to raise his right hand. Shakingly, it pointed toward the beautiful girl, his model.

"Natalie," he said, "not Joyce." The last words were a mere choking gurgle, as his head fell forward and his heart ceased to beat.

"No!" Natalie screamed. "No! Eric, don't say—"

But Eric Stannard would say no word again in this world.

Beatrice Faulkner staggered to a divan and sank down among the pillows.

"Do something, Blake," she cried. "Get a doctor. Get Mr. Barry. Call Halpin. Oh, Joyce, what does it all mean?"

Then Mrs. Faulkner forced herself to go to Joyce's assistance, and gently raised her from the floor, where she was still crouching by her husband's side.

"I don't—know—" returned Joyce Stannard, her frightened eyes staring in tearless agony. "Did you kill him, Natalie?"

"No!" cried the girl. "You know I didn't! You killed him yourself!"

Halpin, the butler, came in the room, followed by Miller, who was Stannard's own man.

Astounded, amazed, but not hysterical, these old, trusted and capable servants took the helm.

"Telephone for Doctor Keith," Miller told the other, "and then find Mr. Barry."

Barry Stannard was Eric's son by a former marriage; a boy of twenty, of lovable and sunny disposition, and devoted to his father and to his young stepmother. He soon appeared, for he had been found strolling about the grounds.

He came in at Halpin's message, and seeing the still figure in the armchair, sprang toward it, with a cry. Then, as suddenly, he turned, and without a word or glance at any one else, he ran from the room.

Without touching it further than to assure himself that life was really extinct, Miller stood, a selfappointed sentinel over the body of his dead master. He looked curiously at the instrument of death, but said no word concerning it.

There was more or less confusion. Several servants, both men and women, came to the doors, some daring to enter, but except in one or two instances, Miller ordered them out.

Annette, Mrs. Stannard's maid, he advised to look after the ladies, and Foster, a houseman, he detailed to keep an eye on Barry.

"Where is Mr. Barry?" asked the man.

"I don't know," returned Miller, calmly. "He just stepped out—probably he's on the terrace. Don't annoy him by intrusion, but be near if he wants you."

The three women of the household said almost nothing. Mrs. Faulkner was so stupefied by the situation, and the inexplicable attitude in which she had found her hostess and the girl, Natalie, she could think of nothing to say to either. And the two who had stood near the dying man, as the light disclosed the group, were equally silent.

Annette proffered fans and sal volatile impartially to all three, but she, also, though usually too voluble, had no words.

After what seemed an interminable wait, Dr. Keith arrived.

"Stabbed," he said, briefly, as he examined the body, "and with one of his own etching needles! Who did it?"

"With what?" exclaimed Mrs. Faulkner, looking puzzled.

"With an etching point—or needle. An artist's tool. Who did it?"

There was a silence, not so much awkward, as fraught with horror. Who could answer this question, even by a surmise.

Blake threw himself into the breach.

"We don't know, sir," he said. "It was doubtless done in the dark, and, when I turned up on the lights—the—the murderer had fled."

A half exclamation from Joyce seemed to deny this assertion, and Natalie's lovely face again showed that hunted, terrified look that had marked it at first.

"Where's Barry?" went on Dr. Keith.

"I am here," said young Stannard, himself, coming in from the terrace. "Dr. Keith, I want this matter hushed up. I am master here now, and horrible though it may all be, it will not lessen our trouble, but rather increase it, if you have any investigation or inquiry made into this thing."

Dr. Keith looked at the speaker in amazement. "You don't know what you're talking about, Barry, my boy. It is not possible to ignore the facts and causes of an occurrence of this sort. Do you know who stabbed your father?"

"No, I do not. Nor do I want to know. Father is gone, no persecution of any innocent person can restore him to life, and the criminal can never be found."

"Why not? Why do you say that?"

"I feel sure of it. Oh, listen to me, Dr. Keith. Be guided by my wishes, and do not seek the one who brought about my father's death. Joyce, you agree with me, don't you?"

The young fellow had never addressed his father's wife more formally than this; indeed, there was not much more than half a dozen years between their ages, and Joyce, at twenty-seven or thereabouts, looked almost as young as her stepson. There had always been good comradeship between the two, and during the two years Joyce had been Stannard's wife she and Barry had never had a word of disagreement or unpleasantness of any sort.

About six weeks ago, Natalie Vernon, a professional model, had come to pose for Stannard, and as she had proved most satisfactory, Eric had informed his wife that he wished the girl to stay as a house guest for a time. Joyce had voiced no objection, whatever she may have felt in her heart, and had always treated Natalie with all courtesy and kindness.

The girl was a most exquisite beauty, a perfect blonde, with a face like Dresden china and a form of fairylike grace. The soft pink and white of her apple-blossom skin, the true sky colour of her eyes and the gleaming gold of her wonderful hair were Greuze-like in their effects, yet of an added piquancy and charm.

It is not to be wondered at that Barry promptly fell in love with her, nor is it remarkable that Eric himself was more or less under the spell of his beautiful model. A worshipper of all beauty, Stannard could not help it if his soul bowed down to this masterpiece of Nature's.

A professional model Natalie was, but only for the draped figure. She was but eighteen, had been well brought up and educated, but, obliged to earn her own living, had found she had no resources of work except in her God-given beauty. Posing was a joy to her, and she had posed for but a few artists and those of the better, even best class. But Eric, accustomed to having whatever he desired, was determined Natalie should pose for some allegorical figures in a great picture on which he was engaged. This she refused to do, and the more Stannard insisted the more obdurate she became, until there was continual war between them on the subject. And owing to this state of things, Natalie had decided she must leave "Faulkner's Folly," and it was only Barry's entreaties that had thus far kept her from fulfilling her intentions.

Joyce, herself a beautiful woman, of the darkhaired, brown-eyed type, had often been a model for Eric's pictures, and if she resented being superseded by this peaches and cream maiden, she never confided the fact to those about her. Joyce Stannard was clever by nature, and she knew the quickest way to make her impressionable husband fall desperately in love with Natalie, was for her, his wife, to be openly jealous. So this Joyce would not appear to be. She chaffed him gaily about his dollfaced model and treated Natalie with the patronising generosity one would show to a pretty child.

But if Joyce was clever, Natalie was too, and she took this treatment exactly as it was offered, and returned it in kind. Her manner to her hostess was entirely correct, well-bred and even indicative of gratitude; but it also implied, with subtle touch, the older and more settled state of Joyce, and gave a hint of contrast in the freshness of Natalie's extreme youth and the permissibility of a spice of the madcap in her ways.

But all these things, on both sides, were so veiled, so delicately suggested, that they were imperceptible to any but the closest observer.

And now, whatever the facts of Eric Stannard's death might be shown to be, now it must soon be made known that when the lights of the room where he died were turned on, they had revealed these two —his wife and his paid model—near his stricken body, already quivering with its last few heartbeats.

In answer to Barry's question, Joyce lifted her white face. "I don't know—" she said, slowly, "I suppose—as Dr. Keith says—these things must be —be attended to in—in the usual way. But I, too, shrink from the awful publicity and the harrowing experience we must go through,— Beatrice, what do you think?"

Mrs. Faulkner replied, with a gentle sympathy: "I fear it won't matter what we think, Joyce, dear. The law will step in, as always, in case of a crime, and our opinions or wishes will count for nothing."

"I have sent for the Coroner and for the Police," said Dr. Keith, who had given Halpin many whispered orders. "Now, Barry, don't be unreasonable. You can no more stop the routine of the law's procedure than the stars in their courses. If you know any facts you must be prepared to state them truthfully. If not, you must say or do nothing that will put any obstacle in the way of proper inquiry."

Dr. Keith was treating Barry like a child, and though the boy resented it, he said nothing, but his face showed his hurt pride and his disappointment.

"Tell us all you can of the facts of the attack," said Beatrice Faulkner to the doctor.

"The simple facts are plainly seen," was the reply. "Some one standing in front of Mr. Stannard, as he sat in his chair, intentionally stabbed him with the etching needle. The instrument penetrated his flesh, just above and a little to one side of the breast bone, piercing the jugular vein and causing almost instant death."

"Could it not have been a suicide?"

"Impossible, Mrs. Faulkner. Stannard could not have managed that thrust, and, too, the position of his hands precludes the theory of suicide. But the Coroner and his physician will, I am sure, corroborate my statement. It is a clear case of wilful murder, for, as you must see for yourself, no accidental touch of that instrument would bring about such a deep sinking of the point in a vital part of the victim."

"But, if I may ask, sir," said Miller, respectfully, "how could a murderer see to strike such a blow in a dark room? While Mr. Stannard could have stabbed himself in the dark."

"Those points are outside my jurisdiction," returned the Doctor, looking grave. "The Coroner and the Police Detectives will endeavour to give the answers to your perfectly logical queries."

And then the men from Police Headquarters arrived.

Chapter 2: Where They Stood

THE countryside was in a tumult. A murder mystery at Faulkner's Folly, of all places in world! Rensselaer Park, the aristocratic Long Island settlement, of which the celebrated house was the star exhibit, could scarcely believe its ears as the news flew about. And the criminal? Public opinion settled at once on an intruder, either burglarious or inimical. Of course, a man of Eric Stannard's position and personality had enemies, as well as friends, from Paris, France, to Paris, Maine. Equally, of course, his enormous collection of valuable art works and even more valuable jewels would tempt robbers.

But the vague rumors as to his wife or that darling little model girl being implicated, were absurd. To be sure, the installation of Miss Vernon as a house guest was a fling in the face of conventions, but Eric Stannard was a law unto himself; and, too, Mrs. Stannard had always introduced the girl as her friend.

The Stannards were comparatively new people at The Park, but Mrs. Faulkner, whose husband had built the Folly, was even now visiting there, and her sanction was enough for the community. It would, one must admit, be thrillingly exciting to suspect a woman in the case, but it was too impossible. No, it was without doubt, a desperate marauder. Thus the neighbours.

But the Police thought differently. The report of the Post Patrolman who first appeared upon the scene of the tragedy included a vivid description of the demeanour of the two ladies; and the whole force, from the Inspector down, determined to discover which was guilty. To them the death of Eric Stannard was merely a case, but from the nature of things it was, or would become, a celebrated case, and as such, they were elated over their connection with it.

In due course, the Coroner's Inquest took place, and was held in the big studio where Eric Stannard had met his death.

Owing to the personality of Coroner Lamson, this was not the perfunctory proceeding that inquests sometimes are, but served to bring out the indicative facts of the situation.

It was the day after the murder and the room was partially filled with the officers of the law, the jury and a crowd of morbidly curious strangers. It seemed sacrilege to give over the splendid apartment to the demands of the occasion, and many of the audience sat timidly on the edge of the luxurious chairs or stared at the multitudinous pictures, statues and artistic paraphernalia. In the original plan the studio had been a ballroom, but its fine North light and great size fitted it for the workroom of the master painter. Nor was the brush the only implement of Eric Stannard. He had experimented with almost equal success in pastel work, he had done some good modelling and of late he had become deeply interested in etching. And it had been one of his own etching needles that had been the direct cause of his untimely death.

This fact was testified to by Doctor Keith, who further detailed his being called to the house the night before. He stated that he had arrived within fifteen minutes after Mr. Stannard—as the family had told him—had breathed his last. Examination of the body had disclosed that death was caused by the piercing of the jugular vein and the weapon, which was not removed until later, was a tool known as an Etcher's needle, a slender, sharp instrument, set in a wooden handle, the whole being not unlike a brad-awl. On being shown the needle, the Doctor identified it as the instrument of death.

Blake, the footman, was next questioned. He was of calm demeanour and impassive countenance, but his answers were alert and intelligent.

"Too much so," thought Mr. Robert Roberts, a Police Detective, who had been put upon the case, to his own decided satisfaction. "That man knows what he's talking about, if he is a wooden-face."

Now, Roberts, called by his chums, Bobsy, was himself alert and intelligent, and therefore recognised those traits in others. He listened attentively as Coroner Lamson put his queries.

"You were the first to discover your master's dead body?"

"Mr. Stannard was not dead when I entered the room,—" replied Blake.

"No, no, to be sure. I mean, you were the first to enter the room after the man was stabbed?"

"That I can't say. When I entered—" Blake paused, and glanced uncertainly about. Barry Stannard was looking at the footman with a stern face.

Inspector Bardon, who was present, interposed. "Tell the story in your own words, my man. We'll best get at it that way."

"I was on duty in the hall," began Blake, slowly, "and I noticed the lights go out in the studio here—"

"Was the door between the hall and studio open?" asked Lamson.

"No, sir, not open, but it was a very little ajar. I didn't think much about the light going out, though Mr. Stannard never turned off the lights when he left the room to go upstairs to bed. And if it did strike me as a bit queer, I had no time to think the matter over, for just then I heard a slight sound,—a gasping like, as if somebody was in distress. As I had not been called, I didn't enter, but I did try to peep in at the crack of the door. This was not curiosity, but there was something in that gasp that—that scared me a little."

"What next?" said the Coroner, as Blake paused.

"Just then, sir, Mrs. Faulkner came down the stairs. She was surprised to see me peeping at a door, and spoke chidingly. But I was so alarmed, I forgot myself, and— well, and just then, I heard a distinct sound—a terrible, gurgling sound, and a voice said, 'Help!' I turned to Mrs. Faulkner to see if she had heard it, and she had, for her face looked frightened and she asked me what it meant, and she told me to go in and turn on the light. So —so, I did, and then I saw—"

"Be very careful now, Blake; tell us exactly what you saw."

"I saw Mr. Stannard first, at the other end of the room, in his favourite big chair, and he was like a man dying—"

"Have you ever seen a man die?" Lamson snapped out the words as if his own nerves were at a tension.

"No—no, sir."

"Then how do you know how one would look?"

"I saw something had been thrust into his breast, I saw red stains on his shirt front, and I saw his face, drawn as in agony, and his eyes staring, yet with a sort of glaze over them, and his hands stretched out, but sort of fluttering, as if he had lost control over his muscles. I couldn't think other than that he was a dying man, sir."

"That is what I want you to tell, Blake. An exact account of the scene as it appeared to you. Now the rest of it. Were you too absorbed in the spectacle of Mr. Stannard's plight to see clearly the others who were present?"

"No, sir," and the man's calm face quivered now. "It is as if photographed on my brain. I can never forget it. Behind Mr. Stannard were the two ladies, Mrs. Stannard and Miss Vernon."

"Directly behind him?"

"Not that, exactly. Mrs. Stannard stood behind, but off toward his left, and Miss Vernon was behind, but toward the right."

"Show me exactly, Blake, where these two ladies stood," and Coroner Lamson rose to see his demands fulfilled.

"Oh, sir," begged Blake, his frightened eyes wavering toward the members of the household which employed him, "oh, sir—Mrs. Faulkner, sir,—she came in with me,—she can tell better than I—"

"Mrs. Faulkner will be questioned in due time. You came in first; we will hear your version and then hers. Be accurate now."

With great hesitancy, Blake stepped to the spots he had designated.

"Mrs. Stannard stood here," he said, indicating a position perhaps a yard back and to the left of Stannard's chair, which was still in its place.

"What was she doing?"

"Nothing, sir. One hand was on this table, and the other sort of clasped against her breast."

"And Miss Vernon?"

"She was over here," and Blake, still behind the chair, crossed to its other side, and stood near the outer door.

"How was she standing?"

"Against this small table, and the table was swaying back and forth, like it would upset in a minute."

"And her hands?"

"They were both behind her, sir, clutching at the table."

"You have a wonderful memory, Blake," and the Coroner looked hard at his witness.

"Not always, sir. But the thing is like a picture to my mind."

"Like a moving picture?"

"No, sir, nobody moved. It was like a tableau, sir—"

"And then," prompted Inspector Bardon.

At this point, Barry Stannard was again seen to look at Blake with a glance of deep concentration.

"Important, if true," Detective Roberts said to himself. "Young Stannard is afraid of the footman's further disclosures!"

Whether that was so or not, Blake suddenly lost his power of clear and concise narration.

"Why, then—" he stammered, "then, all was confusion. I started toward Mr. Stannard, it—it seemed my duty. And Mrs. Faulkner, she came toward him—"

"And the two ladies behind him?"

"They came toward him, too, and Mrs. Stannard took hold of his hand—"

"Well?"

"Well, sir, I couldn't help it, sir—I blurted out, 'Who did this?' And Mr. Stannard—he said—"

"Said! Spoke?"

Attention was concentrated on the footman, and it is doubtful if any one save Roberts noticed Barry Stannard's face. It was drawn in an agonised protest at the forthcoming revelation. But Blake, accustomed to obeying orders implicitly, continued to tell his story.

"Yes, sir, he spoke—sort of whispered, in a gasping way—"

"And what did he say?"

"He said, 'Natalie, not Joyce.'"

"You are sure?"

"Yes, sir," answered the stolid Blake. "And he sort of raised his hand, pointing toward the lady." "Pointing toward Miss Vernon, you mean?"

"Yes, sir."

Barry Stannard could stand it no longer. "I won't have this!" he cried. "I won't allow this hysterical story of an ignorant servant to be told in a way to incriminate an innocent girl. It's all wrong!"

The Coroner considered. It did seem too bad to listen to the vital points of the story from an underling, when such tragic issues were at stake.

"Sit down, for the present, Blake," he said. "Mrs. Faulkner, will you give us your version of these events?"

Beatrice Faulkner looked very white and seemed loth to respond and then with a sudden, determined air, she faced the Coroner, and said, "Certainly. Will you ask questions?"

The beautiful woman looked even more stately in her mild acquiescence than she had done on her first mute refusal. Her large, soft black eyes rested on Joyce with a pitying air and then strayed to Natalie, the little model, who was a mere collapsed heap of weeping femininity. With a deep sigh, Beatrice turned to the Coroner.

"I am ready," she said, with the air of one accustomed to dictate times and seasons.

A little awed, Coroner Lamson asked: "Do you corroborate the story as just related by Blake, the footman?"

"Yes, I think so," and the witness drew her beautiful brows together as if in an effort of recollection. Though fully thirty-five, Beatrice Faulkner looked younger, and yet, compared to Joyce or Natalie she seemed a middle-aged matron. "I am sure I agree with his facts as stated, as to our entering the room, but I'm not sure he was able to hear clearly the words spoken by Mr. Stannard. I was not."

"You were not?"

"No. I heard the indistinct mumble of the dying man, but I am not ready to say positively that I clearly understood the words."

"You came down stairs just as Blake was peeping in at the door?"

"He wasn't peeping. He was, it seemed to me, listening. I, naturally, thought it strange to see a footman prying in any way, and I called out his name, reprovingly. Then, I suddenly realised that as he was not my footman I had no right to reprimand him; and just then he turned his full face toward me, and I saw that the man looked startled, and that something unusual must be happening in the studio. He told me the lights had just gone out, and even as he spoke we both heard that sighing 'Help!' It was a fearful sound, and struck a chill to my very heart. I bade Blake turn on the light quickly, and then I followed him into the room."

"Yes, Mrs. Faulkner, that is just as the footman told it. Now, will you tell what you saw in the studio, and what you inferred from it."

"I saw Mr. Stannard in his arm chair, a dagger or some such thing protruding from his breast, and blood stains on his clothing. I inferred that some burglar or marauder had attacked him and perhaps robbed him."

"And how did you think this intruder had entered?"

"I didn't think anything about that. One doesn't have coherent thoughts at such a moment. I realised that he had been stabbed, so of course, I assumed an assailant. Then I saw his wife and Miss Vernon standing near him, and I had no thought save to assist in any way I might. I cried out to Blake to get a doctor, and then I went to Mrs. Stannard's side, just as she was about to faint:"

"Did she faint?"

"No, that is, she did not entirely lose consciousness, though greatly agitated. And then, soon, the butler and Miller, Mr. Stannard's valet, came in, and after that Barry came and—and everything seemed to happen at once. Doctor Keith came—"

"One moment, Mrs. Faulkner, you are getting ahead of your story. What about the words uttered by Mr. Stannard before he died?"

"They were so inarticulate as to be unintelligible."

"You swear this?"

"I do. If he said 'Joyce' or 'Natalie,' it is not at all strange, considering that those two women were in his sight. But I repeat that he did not say them in a connected sentence, nor did he himself mean any real statement. It was the unconscious speech of a dying man. In another instant he was gone."

Though outwardly calm, Beatrice Faulkner's voice trembled, and was so low as to be scarcely audible. But she stood her ground bravely, and her eyes met Barry's for a moment, in the briefest glance of understanding and approval.

"Hum," commented the astute Roberts to his favourite confidant, himself, "the Barry person is in love with the dolly-baby girl, and the queenly lady is his friend, and she's helping him out. She isn't telling all she knows, or if she is, she's colouring it to save the implicated ladies."

"What is your position in this house, Mrs. Faulkner?"

The faintest gleam of amusement passed over the white face. It was almost as if he thought her a housekeeper or governess.

"I am a guest," she returned, simply. "I have been staying here a few weeks for the purpose of having my portrait painted by Mr. Stannard."

"You previously owned this house, did you not?"

"My late husband, an architect of note, built it. Later, it was sold to Mr. Stannard, who has lived in it nearly two years."

"Where were you just before you came down the stairs and saw Blake?"

"In the Drawing Room, on the second floor, at the other end of the house. I had been entertaining a guest, and as he had just taken leave, I went down stairs to rejoin my hostess."

"Where did you expect to find Mrs. Stannard?"

"Where I had left her, in the Billiard Room."

"You left her there? How long before?"

"An hour or so. There were several guests at dinner, and they had drifted to the various rooms afterward."

"Who were the guests at dinner?"

"Mr. Wadsworth, who was with me in the Drawing Room; Mr. Courtenay, a neighbour, and Mr. and Mrs. Truxton, who also live nearby."

"Mrs. Truxton, the jewel collector?"

"Yes; that is the one."

"There was no one else at dinner?"

"Only the family group; Mr. and Mrs. Stannard, Mr. Barry Stannard, Miss Vernon and myself."

"Once again, Mrs. Faulkner, you attach no significance to the words, 'Natalie, not Joyce,' which Blake quotes Mr. Stannard as saying?"

Taken thus unexpectedly, Mrs. Faulkner hesitated. Then she said, steadily: "I do not. They were the articulation of a brain already clouded by approaching death. He merely named the people he saw nearest to him."

"That is not true! Eric meant what he said!"

It was Joyce Stannard who spoke.

CHAPTER 3: WHAT THEY SAID

WITH a vague idea of taking advantage of a psychological moment, Coroner Lamson began to question Joyce. "Why do you make that statement, Mrs. Stannard?" he said; "do you realise that it is a grave implication?"

But Joyce, though not hysterical, was at high tension, and she said, talking rapidly, "My husband's words were in direct answer to the footman's question. Blake said, 'Who did this?' and Mr. Stannard, even pointing to Miss Vernon, said, 'Natalie, not Joyce.' Could anything be plainer?"

"It might seem so, yet we must take into consideration the fast clouding intellect of the dying man, and endeavour thus to get at the truth. Will you tell the circumstances of your entering the room, Mrs. Stannard?"

"Of course I will. I had been in the Billiard Room for some time, ever since dinner, in fact—"

"Alone?"

"Not at first. Several were there with me. Then, later, all had gone—and—I was there alone."

The speaker paused. She seemed to forget her audience and became lost in recollection or in thought. She looked very beautiful, as she sat, robed in her black gown of soft, thin material, with a bit of white turned in at the throat. Her brown hair waved carelessly back to a loose, low knot and her deep-set brown eyes, full of sorrow, grew suddenly luminous.

"Perhaps it wasn't Natalie," she said, speaking breathlessly. "Perhaps it wasn't Miss Vernon— after all."

"We are not asking your opinion, Mrs. Stannard," said the Coroner, stiffly; "kindly confine your recital to the facts as they happened."

But now, the witness' poise was shaken. Of a temperamental nature, Joyce Stannard had thought of something or realised something that affected the trend of her testimony.

Bobsy Roberts watched her with intense interest. "Well, Milady," he said to her, mentally, "you've struck a snag in your well-planned defence. Careful now, don't leap before you look!"

"Yes," said Joyce, but her quivering lip precluded further speech.

The Coroner was made decidedly uncomfortable by the sight of her beauty and her distress, always a disquieting combination, and to hide his sympathy, he repeated, brusquely, "The facts, please, as they occurred."

"I was in the Billiard Room," Joyce began again, "and I heard, in the studio, a slight sound of some sort, and then the light in here went out."

"Which was first, the sound or the sudden darkness?"

"The sound—no, the darkness. I don't really know. Perhaps they were simultaneous."

"One moment; was the Billiard Room lighted?"

"Yes."

"And the door between open?"

"The sliding doors were open—the curtains pulled together."

Glancing at the heavy tapestry curtains in question, Mr. Lamson said quickly: "If they were pulled together, and the room where you were was light, how could you notice when this room went dark?"

Joyce looked bewildered. "I don't know," she said, blankly, "how could I?"

The question was so naive, and the brown eyes so puzzled and troubled, that Bobsy Roberts whistled to himself. But not for want of thought. His thoughts flocked so fast he could scarcely marshal them into line. "Of course," his principal thought was, "one of these women is guilty. If the crime had been committed by a burglar they wouldn't have any of this back and forth with their eyes. Now, the question is, which one?"

Joyce and Natalie had exchanged many glances. But to a stranger they were unreadable, and Roberts contented himself with storing them up in his memory for future consideration. And now, as Joyce looked confused and nonplussed, Natalie seemed a bit triumphant, but she as quickly drooped her eyes and veiled whatever emotion they showed.

"But you are sure you did know when the studio lights went out?" pursued Lamson.

"Why, yes—I think so. You see—it was all so confused—"

"What was?"

"Why,—the lights,—and that queer sound— and—"

"Go on, Mrs. Stannard. Never mind the lights and the sound. You entered the studio from the Billiard Room, and saw?"

"I didn't see anything!" declared Joyce, with a sudden toss of her head. "I c-couldn't. It was dark, you know. Then somebody, Blake, you know, turned the switch, and I saw Miss Vernon standing by my dying husband's—"

"How did you know he was dying? Did you see Miss Vernon strike the blow?"

"No. But she was in the room when I entered— and, too, Eric said it was Natalie and not—me."

"You are prepared to swear that Miss Vernon was in the room before you were?"

"She was there when I went in."

"But it was dark, how could you see her?"

"I didn't. I heard her breathing in a quick, frightened way."

"And when you first saw her?"

"She was cowering back against the little paint stand."

"Looking terrified?"

"Yes, and—"

"And what?"

"And guilty." Joyce said the words solemnly, as one unwillingly pronouncing a doom.

"Mrs. Stannard, I must be unpleasantly personal. Can you think of any reason why Miss Vernon would desire your husband's death?"

Joyce trembled visibly. "I cannot answer a question like that," she said, in a low tone.

"I'm sorry,—but you must."

"No, then," and Joyce looked squarely at Natalie. "I cannot imagine why she should desire his death. I certainly cannot."

"But any reason why she should dislike him, or wish him ill?"

"N-no."

"Think again."

"My husband was a great artist," Joyce began, as if thinking it out for herself. "He was accustomed to having his models do as he requested. Miss Vernon was not always amenable to his wishes and—and they were not very good friends."

"But you and Miss Vernon are good friends? You like her?"

Joyce favoured Natalie with a calm stare. "Certainly," she said, in an even voice, "I like her."

"Whew!" breathed dur friend Roberts, silently. "At last I see what one Mr. Pope meant when he wrote:

"Damn with faint praise, assent with civil leer,
And, without sneering, cause the rest to sneer."

For, surely, Joyce's attestation of friendship between herself and the artist's model convinced nobody. She sat, gracefully erect, her serious face blank of any emotion, yet impressing all with the sense of profound feeling beneath.

"In what ways did Miss Vernon incur Mr. Stannard's displeasure?" asked Lamson.

"Merely on some technical matters connected with her posing for his pictures," was the nonchalant reply.

"That, then, could scarcely be construed into a motive for murder?"

"Scarcely." Joyce seemed to give a mere parrot-like repetition of the Coroner's word.

"Yet, you are willing to believe that Miss Vernon is the criminal we are seeking?"

"I do not say that," and Joyce spoke softly. "I can only say I saw her here when I came into this room and found my husband dying."

"Might she not have come in just as you did, attracted by that strange sound, as of a man in pain?"

"In that case, who could have stabbed my husband? There was no one else near. That has been testified by those who entered at the other end of the room."

"Could not a burglar have entered by a window, attempted robbery, and, being discovered, stabbed Mr. Stannard in self-preservation?"

"How could he have entered?" said Joyce, dully.

"I can see no way. That is, he might have been in here, but in no way could he have gotten out. That great North window, I am told, opens only in a few high sectional panes. It is shaded by rollers from the bottom, and is inaccessible. The other large window, the West one, is so blocked up with easels, canvases and casts, that it is certain nobody could get in or out of that. The door to the main hall was, of course, in full sight of Blake the footman, and that leaves only the South end of the room to be considered. Now no intruder could have gone out by the door to the Billiard Room or the door to the Terrace without having been seen by you or Miss Vernon, who claims she was on the Terrace all evening."

Every one present looked around at the Studio. They saw a spacious room, about forty feet long by thirty wide, its lofty ceiling fully twenty feet high. An enormous fireplace was on the side toward the house, and above it ran an ornamental balcony, reached by a light staircase at either end. The fine, big windows were of stained glass, save where ground glass had been put in to meet the artist's needs. Originally a ballroom, the decorations were ornate but in restrained and harmonious taste. There were priceless rugs on the floor, priceless works of art all about, and furnishings of regal state and luxury. Yet, also, was there the litter and mess of working materials and mediums—seemingly inseparable from any studio, however watched and tended. Here would be a stunning Elizabethan chair, all carved wood and red velvet, heaped high with paintboxes and palettes; there, an antique chest of marvellous workmanship, from whose half-open lid peeped bits of rare drapery stuffs or quaintly fashioned garments. Tables everywhere, of inlay or marquetry, were piled with sketches, boxes of pastels, or small casts. Jugs and vases, fit only for museum pieces, held sheafs of paint-brushes, while scores of canvases, both blank and painted, stood all round the wall.

The armchair, in which Eric Stannard had sat when he died, was undisturbed, also the tables near it. A new idea seemed to strike Lamson. He said, "When you came in in the darkness, Mrs. Stannard, how did you avoid stumbling over the chairs and stands in your way? I count four of them, practically in the course you must have pursued."

Joyce looked at the part of the room in question. True, there were four or more small pieces of furniture that would have bothered one coming in without a light.

"That's so!" she said, as if the idea were illuminating. "I must have come in just after or at the very moment that Blake lighted the electrics!"

"And found Miss Vernon already here?"

"Yes," said Joyce.

"Miss Vernon, will you tell your story?" said Lamson, abruptly, turning from Joyce to the girl.

"Why—I—" Natalie fluttered like a frightened bird, and gazed piteously at the inquisitor. "I don't know how."

"Good work!" commented Bobsy Roberts, mentally. "Smart little girl to know how the baby act fetches 'em!"

But if Natalie Vernon's air of helplessness was assumed, it was sufficiently well done to convince all who saw it.

"Poor little thing!" was in everybody's mind as the rosebud face looked pleadingly at the Coroner. At that moment, if she had declared herself the guilty wretch, nobody would have believed her.

Lamson's abruptness vanished, and he said, gently, "Just a simple description, Miss Vernon, of your presence in this room last night."

"It was this way," she began, and her face drew itself into delicious wrinkles, as she chose her words. "I had been, ever since dinner, almost, on the terrace."

"Alone?"

"Oh, no. Different people were there. Coming and going, you know. Well, at last, I chanced to be there alone—"

"Who had been with you latest?"

"Let me see," and the palpable effort to remember was too pronounced to be real, "I guess—yes, I'm sure it was Barry,—Mr. Barry Stannard. And he went away—"

"Where?"

"I don't know. For a stroll with the dogs, probably. I was about to go upstairs to my room, when I heard a sound in the studio that seemed queer."

"How, queer?"

"As if somebody were calling me—I mean, calling for somebody."

"Did you hear your name?" and Lamson caught at the straw.

"Oh, no, just a general exclamation, it was. And I went toward the door to listen, if it might be repeated."

"Was the door open?"

"No, but it has glass in it, with sash curtains, and these were a little way open, and I could see through them that the light went out suddenly—"

"Well?"

"And then I went right in, without making a sound—"

"Didn't it make a sound as you opened the door?"

"The door was open."

"You said it was not."

"Oh, I don't know whether it was or not! I was so scared to see Eric,—Mr. Stannard, dead or dying, and his wife standing there as if she had just—"

"Just what? Killed him?"

"Yes," and Natalie's big blue eyes were violet with horror. "She had! And she stood there, just as Blake said, one hand on the table, and one clutched to her breast. She did do it, Mr. Coroner. She must have been out of her mind, you know, but she did it, for I saw her."

"Saw her kill him?"

"No, not that. But I saw her just after the deed was done, and she was the picture of guilty fear!" If Natalie could have been transferred to canvas as she looked then, the picture would have made any painter's fortune. The girl was in white, soft, crepy wool stuff, that clung and fell in lovely lines, for the gown had been designed by no less a genius than Stannard himself. It was his whim to have Natalie about the house in the gowns in which he posed her, that he might catch an occasional unexpected effect. But the simple affair was not out of place as a morning house-gown, and more than one woman in the audience took careful note of its cut and pattern. Her golden hair was carelessly tossed up in a mass of curls, held with one hair-pin, a huge amber thing, that threatened every minute to slip out, and one couldn't help wishing it would. Her wonderful eyes had long dark lashes, and her pink cheeks were rosy now, because of her nervous excitement. So thin was her delicate skin that her hands and throat were flushed a soft pink and her curved lips were scarlet. Yet notwithstanding the marvellous colouring, there was not one iota of doubt that it was Nature's own. The play of rose and white in her cheeks, the sudden occasional paling of the red lips and the perfection of the tiny shreds of curl that clustered at her throbbing temples all spoke of the real humanity of this girl's beauty. Small wonder the artist wanted her for his own pictures exclusively! Joyce was a beautiful woman, but this child, this fairy princess, was a dream, a very Titania of charm and wonder.

Not by her testimony, not by words of assertion, but by her ethereal, her incredible beauty, this wonder-girl took captive every heart and, without effort, secured the sympathy and belief of everybody present.

And yet, the Coroner had to do his duty. Had to say, in curt, accusing tones, "Then how do you explain Mr. Stannard's dying words, 'Natalie, not Joyce!'?"

The red lips quivered, the roseleaf cheeks grew pinker and great tears formed in the appealing blue eyes.

"Don't ask me that!" she cried; "oh, pray, don't ask me that!"

"But I do, I must ask you. And I must ask you why you stabbed him? Had he asked you to pose in any way to which you were unwilling to consent? Had he insisted, after you refused? Was he tyrannical? Brutal? Cruel? Did you have to defend yourself? Was it on an impulse of sudden anger or indignation?"

"Stop! Stop!" cried Natalie, putting her pink finger tips into her tiny, rosy ears. "Stop! He was none of those things! He was good to me, he —he—"

"Good to you, yet you killed him! Kind to you, yet you took his life—"

"I didn't! I tell you I didn't! It was Joyce! She—"

"Miss Vernon, if you came into the room in the dark, how could you effect an entrance without upsetting something? There are even more small racks and stands on that side of the room than the other."

"No, I didn't upset anything—" and Natalie stared at him.

"Then you came in before the room was darkened,— long before,—and you darkened it yourself, after you had driven the blow that ended the life of your friend and patron."

Coroner Lamson paused, as the dawn-pink of Natalie's face turned to a creamy pallor, and the girl sank, unconscious, into a chair.

"Brutal!" cried Barry Stannard, springing to her side. "Inexcusable, Mr. Lamson. This is no place for a Third Degree procedure!" and asking no one's permission, he carried the slight form from the studio.

CHAPTER 4: GOLDENHEART

A MURMUR of indignation sounded faintly through the room. Public Opinion was not with the Coroner, however black the case might look against the pretty little model. For "model," Natalie was always called, in spite of the fact that she was an honoured guest in the Stannard's house. And she looked like a model. Her manners, though correct in every way, were not those of an ingenuous flapper or a pert debutante. She had the poise and assurance of a woman of the world, with the appearance of an innocent, rather than ignorant, child. But her self-reliance, though it had given way before the Coroner's accusation, was always evident in the clear gaze of her apprehending eyes and the set of her lovely head. Moreover, she had that precious possession called charm to an infinite degree. It was the despair of the artists who had painted her, and Eric Stannard, Unwilling to be baffled, had tried a hundred times, more or less successfully, to fasten that charm in colour medium. Of late, he had tried it in his etching. An unfinished piece of work was a waxed plate bearing an exquisite portrayal of Natalie as Goldenrod. This he had previously painted, and the result, a study in yellow, was his copy for the etching. The canvas showed the girl, her arms full of goldenrod, her yellow gown and her yellow hair against a background of yellow autumn leaves. It was a masterpiece, even for Stannard. And aside from the colour, the lines were so beautiful that he decided to make an etching of the study.

The waxed plate, with this design, had been found on the floor near Eric's chair, after his death. The wax had been scratched and smudged, quite evidently by some furious hand, and the scratches and disfigurements were doubtless made by the very instrument that had caused the artist's death.

This was indicative, beyond a doubt; but what was indicated? That Natalie, in a fit of anger at Eric, had destroyed his picture of her? Or, that Joyce, in a jealous rage, had resented the portrait?

The painting, as Natalie had posed for it, was a lovely girl in a full flowing robe of soft, opaque stuff, showing only a bit of throat and shoulder, and one rounded arm. The etching, as the artist had drawn it, garbed the figure in a filmy, transparent drapery, revealing lines that gave a totally different character to the work.

Natalie Vernon was a prude, there was no denying that. Whether she was absurdly fanatical on the subject or not, was her own affair. But could an indignant girl go so far as to kill an artist who had drawn her in a way she didn't care to be portrayed? It was most unlikely. Still, there was latent fire in those blue eyes, there was force of character in those curved scarlet lips, and if Miss Vernon chose to be an unusual, even eccentric model, she was important enough to make her own terms and insist upon them. And in a furious moment of surprised indignation, what might not a woman do?

Again, could it not be that the artist's wife had had her jealousy stirred to its depths by this latest result of her husband's interest in the model? Could she not, coming upon him as he mused over his drawing on the wax, have snatched the etching tool from his table and revenged her slighted wifehood?

"It's a poor clue that won't work both ways," mused Bobsy Roberts, as he heard of this etching business. The story of it had been told while Natalie was out of the room. Joyce listened with an unruffled countenance. Either she was uninterested, or determined to appear so.

Coroner Lamson next called as witnesses the guests who had been at dinner the night before.

The first, a Mr. Wadsworth, told a straightforward story of the occasion. He was a genial, pleasant man, a neighbour and a widower.

After dinner, he stated, he had been for a time with his host and others in the studio. Mr. Stannard had shown some new gems, a recent addition to his collection. After that, Mr. Wadsworth had gone to the Billiard Room, and later, he and Mrs. Faulkner had gone to the Drawing Room at the other end of the house. He had remained there with the lady until perhaps half past eleven—"

"Wait," interposed the Coroner. "Mrs. Faulkner came downstairs, after your departure, at that hour."

"Then it must have been a little earlier. I didn't note the time. I went directly home, and retired without looking at the hour."

"You went out at the front door?"

"Yes; Blake, the footman, let me out. I didn't look for my hostess as I left, for we are on intimate neighbourly terms, and often ignore the formalities."

There was nothing more to be learned from this witness, and the next was Mr. Eugene Courtenay.

But one swift, intense glance passed between Courtenay and Joyce as the witness took the stand. It was seen by no one but the keen-eyed Bobsy, and to him it was a revelation.

"Oh, ho," was his self-communing, "sits the wind in that quarter? Now, if his nibs and the stately chatelaine are—er—en rapport—it puts a distinctly different tint on the racing steed! I must see about this."

Eugene Courtenay was a man of the world, about thirty years old, and a near neighbour. He had been a suitor of Joyce's before she succumbed to Stannard's Cave Man wooing, and since, had been a friend of both.

Easily and leisurely Courtenay gave his testimony, which was to the effect that after the dinner guests had scattered into the various rooms, he had been in the Billiard Room until he went home. Several others had been there, but had drifted away, and he was for a time alone there with his hostess. Then he had taken leave, going out from the Billiard Room, which had an outside door. He had not gone directly home, but had sauntered across a lawn, and had sat for a short time on a garden seat, smoking. He had chanced to sit facing the studio South window, and had noticed the light go out in that room. He thought nothing of it, nor when, a few moments later the room was relit, did he think it strange in any way. Why shouldn't people light and relight their rooms as they chose? He then went home, knowing nothing of the tragedy and heard nothing of it till morning. No further questioning brought out anything of importance and Courtenay was dismissed.

Mr. and Mrs. Truxton gave no new information.

They told of the dinner party, and of the hours afterward. Mr. Truxton mentioned the jewels exhibited by Eric Stannard, and dilated slightly upon them with the enthusiasm of a gem lover, but neither he nor his wife could shed any light on the mystery.

"Where are these jewels?" asked Lamson, suddenly, scenting a possible robbery.

"I don't know," Joyce answered, listlessly. "Mr. Stannard kept some of them in Safety Deposit and some in the house. He had a place of concealment for them, but I preferred not to know where it is. When I wished to wear any of the jewels he got them for me, and afterward put them away again."

"Do you not think, Mrs. Stannard, that a burglar intent on securing these gems might have attempted a robbery, and—"

"Come, come, Lamson," interposed Inspector Bardon, "a burglar would scarcely make his attempt while the household was still up, the house alight, and people sauntering through the grounds."

"No, of course not," responded the Coroner, in no wise abashed.

Next, Barry Stannard was asked to tell what he could of the whole matter.

"It was the work of a burglar," said young Stannard, confidently; "it simply shows his cleverness that he chose a time when he could effect an entrance easily. He need not have been a rough customer. He may have been of a gentlemanly type,— even in evening clothes. But he gained access to my father, I haven't the slightest doubt, and brought to bear some influence or threat that he hoped would gain him his end. When my father refused his demands,—this is my theory and belief,— he either feared discovery or, in a rage of revenge, killed my father with the nearest weapon he could snatch at."

"And then, you think, Mr. Stannard, that this intruder turned off the lights and made his exit just before the ladies entered the room?"

"I do. He was evidently a cool hand, and made a quick and clever getaway."

"And just how did he leave the room? You know, Mrs. Stannard was in the Billiard Room and Miss Vernon on the Terrace, while Blake was at the main hall door."

"He made his escape by the large West window," replied Barry. "If you will examine it on the outside, you will see. the marks of the jimmy, or whatever you call the tool that burglars open windows with."

An officer was sent at once to investigate this, and returned with the information that there certainly were marks and scratches outside the window in question. It was a long, French window, opening like a double door, and near the lock were the telltale marks.

Bobsy Roberts cast one comprehensive glance at the West window, and then closed and reopened one of his rather good-looking grey eyes. He glanced at Barry, and observed, silently, "Some scheme!" after which, he calmly awaited developments.

"But how can we think that a man entered at that window," said Lamson, "when we notice how it is filled with furniture and apparatus?"

"It might have been managed," asserted Barry.

And then Bobsy Roberts spoke out loud. "It couldn't be," he said, positively. "No one could, by any chance or skill, come in or go out by that window without moving those plaster casts that are on the floor. No one could do it without overturning that small easel, whose leg is directly in the path of the window frame as it swings back. If you will try it, Inspector, you will see what I mean."

It was true. Even though the window might be opened, it would crash into and knock over the small, light-weight easel, which held an unfinished picture on a mounted canvas. And it would also knock down some casts which leaned against it.

Barry looked crestfallen, the more so, that now the Coroner regarded him with a sort of suspicion.

"Mr. Stannard," he said, "I don't want to do you an injustice, but your theory is so suspiciously implausible, that I can't help thinking you might have made those scratches on the window yourself, for the purpose of diverting suspicion."

"I did," Barry blurted out, almost like a schoolboy. "And I am not ashamed of it. My father's death is a mystery. So much of a one that I feel sure it will never be solved. For that reason, I did and do want to turn your mind away from the absurd and utterly unfounded presumption you make that the crime could have been committed by either of the two ladies who, hearing my father's dying struggles, rushed to his assistance."

"That may be the case," said Lamson, with one of the ladies you refer to. But the other is, to all appearances the one responsible for the crime. It is my duty to prove or disprove this, even though the position and high character of the ladies make it seem impossible."

"It is impossible!" protested Barry. "I know of facts and conditions which make it possible and probable that an outsider, a—well, a blackmailer, perhaps,—might have attacked my father. This is outside of discovery or proof, but I request,—I demand that you cease to persecute your present suspects!"

The boy, for in his passionate tirade he seemed even younger than usual, quivered with the tensity of his emotion and faced the Coroner with a belligerent antagonism that would have been funny in a case less grave.

Roberts regarded him with interest. "Some chap!" he thought. "I wonder, now, if he did it himself,—and is trying to scatter the scent. No, I fancy it's his fear for the dolly-baby girl, and he jimmied the door in a foolish attempt to make a noise like a burglar."

"Do you know where your father kept his jewels?" asked Lamson, suddenly, and Barry started, as he said, "No, I've no idea. That is, the ones in the house. The others are in deposit with the Black Rock Trust Company."

"Who does know the whereabouts of those kept in the house?"

But nobody seemed to know. Joyce had said she did not. Barry disclaimed the knowledge. Inquired of, Miller, the valet, did not know. Nor Halpin, the old Butler, nor any of the other servants.

It would seem that Eric Stannard had concealed his treasures in a hiding-place known only to himself. An officer was sent to search his personal rooms, and in the meantime Joyce was subjected to a further grilling.

Exhausted by the nervous strain, her calm, handsome face was pale and drawn. Wearily, she answered questions that were not always necessary or tactful.

At last, when Lamson was trying to draw from her an account of what she was doing or thinking after Courtenay had left her alone in the Billiard Room, she seemed to lose both patience and control, and burst forth, impulsively, "I was listening at the Studio door!"

"Ah! And what did you hear?"

"I heard my husband say, 'No, no, my lady, I will not divorce Joyce for you!' and then he laughed,—a certain laugh of his that I always called the trouble laugh,—a sarcastic, irritating chuckle, enough to exasperate anybody,—anybody, beyond the point of endurance!"

The Coroner almost gasped, but fearing to check the flow of speech that promised so much, he said, quietly, "Did you hear anything further?"

"I did. I heard him say, I'll give you the emeralds, if you like, but I really won't marry you.'"

"Your husband was not a cruel man, Mrs. Stannard?"

"On the contrary, he was gentleness itself. He was most courteous and gallant toward all, but if any one went counter to his wishes or opinions, he invariably used a good-natured, jeering tone that was most annoying."

"And to whom were these remarks that you overheard, addressed?"

"How can you ask? I was just about to go into the room, as I felt it my right, when, at that very moment, the light was extinguished. I was so surprised at this, that I stood there, uncertain what to do. Then hearing Eric gasp, as if in distress, I pushed the curtain aside and went in. The rest, I have told you."

Joyce sat down, and as she did so, a wave of crimson swept over her face. She looked startled, ashamed, as if she had violated a confidence or told a secret, which she now regretted. Barry sat beside her, and he was looking at her curiously.

Then the man who had been sent to search for the jewels returned. He reported that he had not been able to find any trace of them, but brought a note he had found on Mr. Stannard's writing desk.

Coroner Lamson read the note, and passed it over to Inspector Bardon.

Eventually it was read aloud. It ran thus:

GOLDENHEART:

You have a strange power over me—you can sway me to your will when I am in your presence. But now, alone, I am my own man and my better self protests at our secret.

You know where the jewels are hidden. Take the emeralds, if you like, and forgive and forget Eric.

The note fell like a bombshell. Everybody gasped at this revelation of the artist's intrigue with his model. Joyce turned white to her very lips, and Barry flushed scarlet.

"Call Miss Vernon," commanded the Coroner, abruptly.

Natalie came in, looking lovelier than ever, and quite composed now. Without a word, Lamson handed her the note.

The girl read it, and returned it. Except for the trembling of her lip, which she bit in her endeavour to control it, she was calm and self-possessed.

"Well?" said the Coroner, as gentle toward her now as he had been fierce before, "what does that note to you mean?"

Natalie turned the full gaze of her troubled eyes on him. If her angel face was ever appealing, it was doubly so now, when her drooped mouth and quivering chin told of her desperate distress.

"It is not to me," she whispered.

"That's right," Bobsy Roberts thought; "stick to that, now. It's fine!"

"It was written to you, and left in Mr. Stannard's desk. Where are the emeralds? Where are the other jewels hidden?"

"I do not know. I tell you that letter is not mine."

"Not yours, because you didn't receive it. But it was written to you, and before it was sent, the writer told you, in so many words, the purport of it here in this very room, and in a rage, you killed him."

Natalie stopped her accuser with a gesture of her hand. Her rosy palm lifted in protest, she said, "Why do you believe Mrs. Stannard's story and not mine? What *I* saw in this room was the jealous wife, cowering in an agony of fear and terror at sight of her own crime."

Lamson paused. He remembered that the testimony of the two disinterested witnesses, Mrs. Faulkner and Blake, went to show that these two women were both there, near the victim, within a brief moment of the crime itself. Who should say which was guilty, the jealous wife or the disappointed girl?

And another point. Mrs. Faulkner and Blake had told in detail the succession of events at the critical moment of the turning off the lights, of the cry for help, and of their entrance; might not Joyce have timed her story by this, and claimed an entrance at the same moment? And, also, might not Natalie merely have patterned her recital after that of Joyce? Which woman was guilty?

Chapter 5: Blake's Story

THE sapient gentlemen of the Coroner's Jury concluded, after a somewhat protracted discussion, that Eric Stannard met his death at those convenient and ever available hands of a person or persons unknown. They could not bring themselves to accuse either Joyce or Natalie, because for each suspect they had only the evidence of the other's unsupported story. And Public Opinion, as represented by the citizens of Rensselaer Park, would have risen in a body to protest against a verdict that implicated either or both of these two women. And yet, there were many exceptions. Many of those whose voices were loudest in declaring the innocence of Joyce and Natalie, expressed private views that stultified their statements. And some, wagged their heads wisely, and whispered a thought of Blake. But most stood out strongly for the burglar theory, ignoring all obstacles in the way of the marauder's entrance, and repeatedly insisting that the non-appearance of the jewels was sufficient proof of robbery. It may be that Barry's self-confessed scratching of the paint on the window-frame turned the trend of thought toward a possible burglar or blackmailer, even if he gained entrance some other way; and it may be this was the loophole through which the two suspected people escaped accusation.

But the interest of the police in these two was strengthened rather than lessened, and their life and conduct were under close scrutiny.

Captain Steele, who had been assigned to the case, declared that he was glad of the verdict, for it was better to have the suspects at large, and he was a firm believer in the principle of giving people sufficient rope and allowing them 'the privilege of hanging themselves.

Captain Steele was at The Folly, as the house was always called,—in spite of the Stannards' attempts to use the more attractive name of Stanhurst, —on the day after the inquest, and Detective Roberts was also there and one or two other policemen and reporters.

Steele had appropriated the small Reception Room next the studio for his quarters, and was going over with great care the reports of the proceedings and evidence of the day before.

"You see, Bobsy," he said, "the burglar stunt won't work. I've tried, and Carter, here, he's tried, and we couldn't come within a mile of getting in or out among that art junk in the window, without making noise and commotion enough to wake the dead."

"I know it," assented Bobsy. "Knew it all the time. Let's cut out Mr. Burglar. Also, Blake was on the door all the evening, and he would have looked in the studio in case of a racket."

"Sure. Now, I want to fix the time of the stab act. They all say about half past eleven, but nobody knows exactly."

"Of course they don't. People in evening togs never know what time it is. Why should they? They don't have to punch a clock. I think the footman would just about know, though. Servants have their hours, you know. And anyway, let's get that man in here."

Blake was summoned, and, though impassive as usual, seemed ready to answer questions.

He retold his story, with no appreciable deviation from what he had testified at the inquest.

"Are you sure it all occurred at half past eleven?" asked Steele.

"Yes, sir. I heard the chimes in the studio just before the light went out."

"How long was the light out?" Roberts put in.

"I should say, not more'n a minute or so. I was that scared when I heard the sounds, I can't tell about the length of time properly. But it wasn't two minutes, I'm sure, between the studio light going off and me turning it on."

"Would you have turned it on, if Mrs. Faulkner hadn't told you to?"

Blake considered. "I can't say. I think, yes, for I heard that 'Help!' distinctly, for all it was so faint. And I think, if I'd been on my own, I'd 'a' gone ahead. At such times a servant has to use his judgment, sir."

"Right you are, Blake," said Bobsy, who had taken a liking to the footman. "Now, tell us all you know of the whereabouts of every member of the family—of the household."

"I don't know much as to that. You see, I was on the hall, and I could only see those who passed through it."

"Well, go clear back, to dinner time, and enumerate them."

"Before dinner, everybody was in the drawing room, that's over the dining room, at the East end of the house. Then they all came down the grand staircase to dinner, and of course I saw them then. After dinner, the ladies had their coffee on the Terrace and the gentlemen stayed at the table. Then, when the men came out of the dining room, they pretty much scattered all over the house. Everybody was in the studio at one time, and then some went to the Billiard Room or in this Reception Room we're now in, or up to the Drawing Room. Then, about eleven, Mr. and Mrs. Truxton went home, and I showed them out. And Mrs. Faulkner and Mr. Wadsworth were in the hall at the same time. But after the Truxtons went, Mrs. Faulkner and Mr. Wadsworth went up to the Drawing Room. You see,—er—"

"What, Blake?"

"Well, if I may say it, sir, he's—er—sweet on her, and they two went off by themselves."

"I see," and Bobsy smiled. "Now, as to the other ladies, Mrs. Stannard and Miss Vernon?"

"Of those I know nothing, for they didn't come around where I was."

"Nor any of the men?"

"No, sir. Well, then, next, Mr. Wadsworth, he came down, and I let him out. He says, 'Good night, Blake,' sort of gay like, and I thought perhaps Mrs. Faulkner had smiled on his suit, sir."

"Very likely. And then, Mrs. Faulkner came down?"

"Yes, but you see, just the moment before, I had heard this queer noise in the studio, and I was listening at the crack of the door. I meant no harm, and no curiosity,—but Mrs. Faulkner came in sight of me just then, and she spoke to me. Then, the lights went out"

"Why, you said they were out before the lady spoke to you."

"Oh, yes, that's right, they were. Well, it's small wonder I get mixed up. They were, sir, because I told Mrs. Faulkner they were, and she said it wasn't my place to comment on that. And she was right, it wasn't my place, to be sure; but I was worried, that's what I was, worried, and then we both heard the cry of 'Help!' and she told me to turn on the studio lights and I did."

"Do they all obey one switch?"

"Yes, sir, that is, there's one main key right at the door jamb that controls all. So when I turned it on, the whole room was ablaze."

"And of course, you couldn't help seeing the exact state of things. Well, Blake, which lady do you think did it?"

"Oh, sir," and Blake's solemn face grew a shade more so, "I couldn't say. I'm sure I don't know. But, it must have been one of them, there's no getting around that. When I saw the three, as you might say, almost in a row, and the two ladies, sir, both near to Mr. Stannard, sir, and both looking— oh, I can't describe how they looked! Why if they were both guilty they couldn't have looked different."

"They weren't both guilty!" cried Roberts. "It couldn't have been collusion, eh, Steele?"

"Nonsense, of course not," returned Captain Steele; "one stabbed him, and the other came in at the sound of his voice. The terror and shock of the culprit and that of the innocent one would both be manifested by the same expressions of horror and fright."

"I believe that," said Bobsy, after a minute's thought. "Now, Blake, as to the actual means of getting in and out of that studio. Let's go in there."

It was rather early in the morning and the members of the household were as yet in their rooms. It was not the intention of the Police to intrude upon them until after the funeral, but it was desirable to make certain inquiries and investigations while the matter was fresh in the minds of the servants.

Roberts intended to interview others of them afterward, but just now Blake was proving so satisfactory that he continued to keep him by.

In the studio, both Steele and Roberts examined carefully the marks on the West window casing.

"Idiot boy!" exclaimed Bobsy. "To think he could fool us into believing this was professional work!"

"It shows a leaping mind on his part, to fly round here and fix it up so quickly," said Steele, a bit admiringly.

"That's what Mr. Barry has, sir, the leaping mind," observed Blake, as if pleased with the phrase. "Often he jumps to a conclusion or decision that his father'd take hours to reach."

"Mr. Stannard was slow, then?"

"Not to say slow, in some things. He was like lightning at his work. But as to a matter, now, that he didn't want to bother about, he would put it off or dawdle about it, something awful."

"And you see," Bobsy went on, "there are only three doors and three windows in the place. Now we have accounted for—"

"What's the gallery for?" asked Steele, gazing up at the gilded iron scrollwork of the ltyle balcony.

"Just for ornament, sir," Blake returned. "And I've heard Mr. Stannard say, it was necessary, to break up that wall. You see, the ceiling is some twenty feet high, and no windows on that side, being next the main house."

"It's all one house,—there's no division?"

"No real division, sir, but this end,—the studio and Billiard Room on this floor, and the rooms directly above,—are all Mr. Stannard's own, and in a way separate from the rest of the house."

"His sleeping room is above the studio?"

"Yes, sir; and his bath and dressing-room and den. Mrs. Stannard's rooms are next, over the Reception Room, and all the other bedrooms are over the dining room end, and in the third story."

"Listen," impatiently cut in Bobsy. "There are six ways of getting in and out. Now nobody could have entered at the hall door where you were, Blake?"

"Oh, no, sir. I was there all the evening, and the hall lighted as bright as day."

"All right. That's one off. Now we'll go round the room. The North window is out of the question, eh?"

"Yes, sir," said Blake, as the query was to him. "It only opens in those high, upper sections, by cords, don't you see?"

Blake showed the contrivance that opened and shut the upper panes, and it was clear to be seen that there was no possibility of entrance that way.

"Next is the West window," Bobsy went on, "and that's settled by a glance. Why, look at the chalk dust on the floor. How could any one walk through that and leave no track?"

This was unanswerable, so they went on to the door to the Billiard Room.

"This is where Mrs. Stannard came in. No other person could have entered this door unless she had seen him. Now, we come to the East window. This was open, I am told, but the wire fly-screen makes it safe. Also, Mr. Courtenay sat on a lawn bench, looking this way, when the light went out. Had a person climbed in at this window before that he must have seen him."

"He couldn't climb in, sir, 'count of the screen," said Blake. "It's not a, movable screen. We put them up for the season, and take them down the middle of October. They all come down next week.

"This door, the last," and Bobsy paused at the door to the Terrace, "is the one at which Miss Vernon entered. If any one else had come in here she would have seen him. That completes our circuit. No one could have gained access to this room except the ones under consideration. Now we are faced by the fact that one of those two women committed the murder, and it's up to us to decide which one."

"There's the fireplace," suggested Steele.

"There was a fire there that night," Blake asserted. "That is, there had been, for the evening was a little chilly, and too, Mrs. Stannard is fond of an open fire. It was burned out when—when it all happened, but the embers were smouldering when I came into the room. And no one could come down the chimney, anyway. It's a crooked flue, and it's full of soot beside."

"No one ever comes down a chimney," said Roberts, "but it's always well to look into it." He peered up into the blackness, but the even coat of soot showed no scratches or marks.

"Then there's no ingress other than those we've noted," Steele mused. "There's no skylight, no cupboards, no doors up in that balcony place," he ran up and across it, as he spoke, tapping on the wainscoted wall. "Solid," he said, as he came down the other little stair. "Now, is there any trap door?"

They lifted rugs and hammered on the floor but the oak was an unmarred surface, and no opening was there of any sort.

"I wanted to be sure," said Roberts, as, a little shamefacedly he pounded on the floorboards around the West window. "Now, I am sure. We have only the two doors to deal with. The door from the Terrace and the one from the studio. Let's look at them both."

Stepping out onto the beautiful covered Terrace, the men paused to take in the glories of the scene. The splendid lawns sloping down to even more splendid gardens were the plan of an artist and a Nature lover both. The October foliage was alight and aglow, and the Autumn flowers were masses of gorgeous bloom. But after a whiff or two of the sunlit morning air, they returned to their quest.

"On this terrace Miss Vernon and Barry Stannard sat until after eleven," Roberts said; "I got that from young Stannard himself."

"Don't put too much faith in those people's ideas of time," warned Steele. "He may think it was after eleven and it may have been much earlier."

"You're right, there. Well, anyway, he sat here with her, in the dark,—he told me had turned off the Terrace light,—and then he went off to give the dogs some exercise. I believe they go for a trot every night, don't they, Blake?"

"Yes, sir; Mr. Barry almost always romps about with the dogs of an evening."

"Well, that leaves Miss Vernon alone here for an indefinite—I mean, an indeterminate time. Now, why doesn't Mr. Courtenay see her, as he sits on that lawn seat yonder?"

"Too dark," said Steele, laconically.

"That's right. She was back, we'll say, under the Terrace roof, and the night was dark. Moreover, the Studio was brightly lighted, also the Billiard Room, which threw the Terrace even more in shadow. Well, then,—I'm sort of reconstructing this,—Miss Vernon sat here, until, as she says, she heard the noise in the studio."

"Or saw the light go out," and Steele shook his head. "Nobody seems to know which happened first, the sudden darkness in there or the queer sound."

"No one knows, except the murderer," said Roberts, seriously. "The murderer knows, because he —or she— turned off the light, but the others, who are innocent, are uncertain about it, as one always is about a moment of unexpected action."

"That's it," and Steele looked at the detective in admiration. "Mighty few can give a clear account of sudden happenings, unless it's a cut and dried account."

"And yet—" Bobsy frowned, "you know both Miss Vernon and Mrs. Stannard became confused about the lights."

"That's because they both tried to copycat the footman's story. You see, the one who really killed Stannard, did shut off the lights, and when she tells her story, and has to stick to it, she gets mixed up about the sound and the lights, because she was in the studio all the time, and not where she says she was, at all. Then, on the other hand, the other of the two, being innocent, gets confused, because she really can't tell just how things did happen."

"Sound enough. Now let's go to the Billiard Room."

Crossing the studio again, they entered the Billiard Room, a large apartment with seats round the walls and the table in the centre.

Cue racks and much smoking and other masculine paraphernalia were all about. There were a skylight of stained glass and a few high side windows. An outside door was on the South side.

"Here Mr. Courtenay left Mrs. Stannard, at much the same time Barry left the girl," Roberts said. "So you see, Steele, their chances are equal."

"Chances of what?"

"I mean chances to go into the studio, unobserved of anybody, commit the deed, turn off the lights, and then, either return to the spot she came from or to remain in the room until the other entered. It must have been that way, for there's no other way for it to be."

"All right; now, what about Mrs. Stannard's story of overhearing the stuff her husband said to the girl?"

"Probably true, but if he said that to Miss Vernon and Mrs. Stannard overheard it, she might have run in and found the dead man, or she might have run in and stabbed the living man."

"In the dark?"

"Perhaps so. She knew where every bit of furniture was. But isn't it quite as likely that the girl did the stabbing?"

"That wax baby?"

"She isn't the baby she looks! Always distrust a blonde."

"But such a blonde!"

"Distrust them in proportion to their blondeness, then. But we've learned all we can here. Back to think it over, and puzzle it out."

CHAPTER 6: MRS. FAULKNER'S ACCOUNT

NOW, although the residents of the aristocratic Rensselaer Park were willing, and even preferred to accept the burglar theory, rather than have more shocking revelations, the newspaper reading public was avid for sensation, and dissatisfied at the failure of the police to arrest anybody, even the hypothetical burglar.

Owing to the prominence of the victim, both socially and in the art world, a great hue and cry was raised for vengeance where vengeance was due. All sorts of theories were propounded by all sorts of people and interest increased rather than dwindled as no definite progress was reported.

Captain Steele was one of the most able men on the force, and his record for success in murder cases was of the best. His reputation was at stake, and he was working his very hardest in his handling of the present matter. His methods were persistent rather than brilliant, and his slowness was often the despair of quick-witted Robert Roberts.

"Captain," Bobsy would say, "do you see that point?"

"I saw it long ago," would be the exasperating reply.

"Well, what about it?"

"I haven't thought it out yet."

"Well, get busy."

"I am busy," the stolid Captain would answer, and go on about his business.

But the two were staunch friends and allies, and possessed the qualities that enabled them to work side by side without friction.

"You see," said Steele, as they were closeted in the Reception Room, "it's more or less a psychological problem."

They liked this room for their confabs. The small size and convenient location suited their purpose admirably. They could shut its two doors, and be entirely secluded or they could open them and get a general idea of what was going on about the house.

"Snug little box," Bobsy had said, when he first saw it, and the walls and ceiling being all of the same general decoration in red and gold, did give it the effect of a well lined box. It was used by the family for the reception of transient callers, and was more formal than the studio or Billiard Room. The Terrace, too, was used as a living place, in available weather, and even now as the two men were deep in their discussion, there could be seen through the south window some servants arranging a small breakfast table out there.

"Psychology is out of my line," Roberts said, in answer to the Captain's assertion.

"Oh, I don't mean anything scientific. But, it's this way. One of those women is lying and one telling the truth. Now, if we tax them with this, we'll get nothing out of them, for they're both at the edge of a nervous breakdown."

"The innocent one, too?"

"Sure. The guilty one is naturally all wrought up, and the innocent one is so scared at the whole thing that she is all in, too. I think the little peach was in love with the artist; I'm not sure of this, but it doesn't matter, anyway. Also, and incidentally, I think that Courtenay man is very much in love with Mrs. Stannard. Now, all these things are none of our business, unless they help us to form conclusions that are our business. And so, we must be rather more tactful and diplomatic than usual, because of dealing with highstrung and fine-calibred natures."

"A murder doesn't connote a high-calibred nature!"

"It may well do so. A strong impulse of revenge or jealousy could, on occasion, sway the highest mind tb the basest deed. Murderers are made, not born, Lombroso to the contrary, notwithstanding.

And it is the coincidence of opportunity and motive that makes crime possible to an otherwise great and noble nature."

"I'm not sure I agree to all that, but if the argument is helpful let's use it by all means."

"It is. Now, here's the situation. As near as I can make out, Mr. Stannard was alone in his studio after the Truxton people had gone; the Faulkner lady and her admirer had gone to the drawing-room, the model was on the Terrace with Barry, and Mrs. Joyce was in the Billiard Room with Courtenay. The trouble is, we don't know how long this interval was. Blake says the Truxtons went at eleven. Well, from eleven, then, till eleven-thirty covers the whole time in question. Between those two moments the crime was led up to and committed."

"Must it have been led up to?"

"Not necessarily, I admit. But suppose, let us say, that soon after eleven, one or other of the two women we're considering, was left alone. Say she came into the studio and had some sort of session with Mr. Stannard that led to the stabbing. Then, say, she turned off the lights, and quickly returned to her post, either in the Billiard Room or on the Terrace, and a moment later, entered again, just as she says she did."

"All right, that goes. Now, which?"

"That's what we must discover by studying the two women, not by hunting clues of a material nature."

"Whichever did it, or whoever did it, had to cross to the other end of the room to turn off the lights, didn't she?"

Captain Steele remembered the switch was near the hall door, and the armchair where Stannard died was at the South end of the room.

"Yes," he agreed, "but that's only a few seconds' work."

"But when she did it, the man was not dead. You know he groaned after the light went out, and later, he spoke."

"Well?"

"Well, can you imagine that little girl having nerve enough for all that? Mrs. Stannard is a much older woman, and a self-possessed one. My opinion leans toward her."

"What about the dying words of the man, and also, what about that letter to the model?"

"There's too much evidence instead of not enough! But before we sift it out, which we can do elsewhere, let's try to learn something more from the people here."

"Servants or the others?"

"The others, if possible. If not, then some servants beside Blake."

The breakfast table on the Terrace had been visited only by Mrs. Faulkner and Barry Stannard. The other ladies had not appeared. The two had quite evidently finished, as the men could see from their lace curtained window, and Roberts proposed they request an interview with one or both of them.

Somewhat to their surprise, the request was graciously granted. Mrs. Faulkner said she should be rather glad of an opportunity to learn what the police had done or were thinking of doing, and Barry seemed anxious to discuss matters also.

But even before they began, Barry was called away on some errand, and Mrs. Faulkner was their only source of information.

Bobsy Roberts was disappointed, for he wanted to talk with a member of the immediate family, but Captain Steele saw a chance to learn something personal of the two women he wished to study.

"You must know, Mrs. Faulkner," began Steele, "that the two women found in the room, near the dying man, are naturally under grave suspicion of guilt. Can you tell us anything that will help clear the innocent or indicate the criminal?"

Beatrice looked at him a moment, before she spoke. She also glanced at Bobsy Roberts, and then, in a low, calm voice she replied: "I think I must remind you that these two women are my dear friends. I have known Mrs. Stannard for years, and Miss Vernon, though a recent acquaintance, is very dear to me. They are both fine, noble women, utterly incapable of the crime, even under deepest provocation. Therefore I do not admit, even to myself, that the circumstances implicate either of them, although they may seem to do so. With this declaration of my attitude in the matter, I will answer any questions that I can, but I will not agree that your theory is the right one."

"Then, who did kill Mr. Stannard?"

"That I cannot say. But in absence of any real evidence against Mrs. Stannard or Miss Vernon, it must seem to have been an intruder of some sort. Though it may not be known how he entered, it is far more easy to believe that he did gain an entrance, than to believe crime of either of those two."

It was plain to be seen Mrs. Faulkner was determined to stand by her friends through thick and thin. So Bobsy started on another tack. "Will you tell us then something of the personal relations of this household? Was Mr. Stannard in love with his pretty model?"

"I think he was," Beatrice rejoined, as if the matter were of no great import, "but Mr. Stannard was the type of man known as a 'lady-killer.' He adored all beautiful women, and was what may be called 'in love' with many. His nature was so volatile and so impressionable, that his love affairs were frequent and ephemeral."

"Mrs. Stannard made no objection to this?"

"I think these queries are unnecessarily personal, but I see, so far, no harm in replying. Mrs. Stannard knew so well her husband's temperament and disposition, that usually she laughed at his sudden adorations, knowing that he tired of them very quickly. The Stannards were a model and a modern couple. They never stooped to petty jealousies or bickerings, and had wide tolerance for each other's actions."

"Mrs. Stannard is his second wife, is she not?"

"Yes, they were married something more than two years ago."

"And Mrs. Stannard had other suitors, who were disappointed at her marriage?"

"That is usually true of any beautiful woman."

"But in her case you know of instances?" Bobsy smiled pleasantly.

"Naturally, as I know her so well."

"And is Mr. Courtenay one of them?"

"Mr. Courtenay was one of her devoted admirers, and since the marriage he has been a friend warmly welcomed here by both Mr. and Mrs. Stannard. No breath of reproach may be brought against Joyce Stannard or Eugene Courtenay. Of this I can assure you."

"And the young lady,—is Barry Stannard a suitor of hers?"

Beatrice's face clouded a little. "Yes; you cannot help seeing that, so I will tell you that he is madly in love with Miss Vernon, but his father strongly objected to the match, and threatened to disinherit Barry if he persisted in his attentions to the girl. I tell you this, because I prefer you to hear the truth from me, rather than a string of garbled gossip."

"And young Stannard persisted?"

"I think so. It was love at first sight on both sides, and Miss Vernon is a very lovely girl,—of quite as lovely a nature as her pure sweet face indicates."

"Might not Mr. Stannard's objection to his son's suit have been prompted by his own admiration for the lovely nature?"

"It might have been," and Beatrice sighed. "Eric Stannard was an exceedingly selfish man, and though his interest in the model was doubtless his usual temporary love affair, it is quite likely that it was the main motive of his displeasure at his son's interference. I am speaking very frankly, for I know these things must all come out, and I am hoping, if you know just how matters are, you will understand the case better and be more prepared to relieve the two women of suspicion."

"It may be so," and Captain Steele nodded his head sagely.

But Mrs. Faulkner was watching him closely. "You are not yet very greatly influenced by my revelations, I can see," she said, "but I am sure you will come around to my way of thinking, sooner or later. The more you see of your suspects, the more you will realise the absurdity of your suspicions."

"That's possibly true: When can we have an interview with either of them?"

"Mrs. Stannard is prostrated. I am sure you cannot see her before the funeral, which will be tomorrow. Won't you refrain from asking it, until after that?"

"Certainly. But Miss Vernon, may we not have a few words with her? You must realise, Mrs. Faulkner, if the girl is innocent, it will be much better for her to see us and answer a few straightforward questions than to appear unwilling to do so."

"I agree with you. I will go and ask her, myself, and advise her to see you. Shall I go now?"

"In a moment, please; but first, one more question. We are trying to discover who last saw Mr. Stannard alive, prior to the time of the murder. What can you tell us as to this?"

"Only that I was in the studio, just before the first of the guests went away. At that time we were all there, I think, except Barry and Natalie, who were out on the Terrace. The two Truxtons went home, and at the same time Mr. Wadsworth and I went up to the drawing room—"

"To be by yourselves?"

A certain kindliness in Bobsy's tone robbed the question of impertinence, and Beatrice smiled a little, as she said, "Yes, exactly. We stayed there perhaps a half hour, and then Mr. Wadsworth went home. I did not go downstairs with him, but sat a moment in the drawing-room,—thinking over some personal matters. Then when I went downstairs, it was to see Blake listening at the door,—and the rest you know."

"Yes; now whom did you leave in the studio, when you and Mr. Wadsworth and the Truxtons went out of it?"

Beatrice thought a moment. "Only Mr. Stannard, his wife and Mr. Courtenay."

"Then Mrs. Stannard and Mr. Courtenay went into the Billiard Room?"

"Yes, and Mr. Stannard went, too. But he went back in the studio,—Joyce told me that,—and he must have been there alone when—the person who killed him came in."

"This would make it, that Mr. Stannard returned to his studio from the Billiard Room at a little after eleven, say, five or ten minutes after. The fact that he cried out for help at about eleven-thirty narrows the time down rather close. We have only about twenty minutes for the intruder to enter and commit the deed. This is long enough if the crime was premeditated, but scarcely giving time for a quarrel or argument to take place."

"Then you assume premeditation?" and Beatrice looked up quickly.

"It would seem so."

"Then I am sure you will find, Mr. Roberts, that it could not have been either of the two you think. For even if one of them might have done such a thing in the heat of passion, neither, I am positive, ever deliberately premeditated it."

"What about the letter found in the desk?"

"That," and Beatrice shook her head emphatically, "that was never meant for Miss Vernon."

"Yet Mrs. Stannard overheard him say practically the same thing to somebody in the studio, a moment or two before the crime was committed."

"Joyce thinks she heard that. But Captain Steele, that poor woman scarcely knew what she was saying at that awful inquest, and she—well, she had reason to think there were women in Mr. Stannard's life, who would be willing,—in fact, who wished him to be divorced from her. She knew this, she knew of that note he had written,—it was not the first of that nature, and she imagined she heard that speech."

"You make Mr. Stannard out a very bad man, Mrs. Faulkner."

"I am sorry to speak ill of the dead, but he was not a good man in the ways we are talking of. In other respects, Eric Stannard had few faults. He was upright, honest and generous. He was kind and he was truthful. And he was extraordinarily brave and honourable. But he was inordinately selfish and of sybaritic instincts. He would not try to curb his admiration for a new and pretty face, and though absolutely loyal to his wife in honour and principle he was a flirt and a gallant, much in the way of a butterfly among the flowers. His genius it is not necessary to speak of. He is known here and abroad as one of the greatest artists of the century. And his wide and varied experiences, his cosmopolitan life and his waywardness of character may well have gained him enemies, who in a secret and clever manner found means to take his life."

"Who will benefit financially by his death?" Captain Steele asked abruptly.

"I haven't heard anything about the will yet, but I'm pretty certain, that outside of a few friendly bequests his fortune is divided between his wife and son, about equally."

"And his jewel collection? Is not that valuable?"

"Very. The emeralds mentioned in that note comprise a fortune in wonderfully matched stones. And there are many more. Yes, it is an exceedingly valuable lot."

"He showed them to Mr. Truxton, that evening?"

"To all of us. That was right after dinner. He showed only a few cases, but of very beautiful stones."

"And then he put them away, where?"

"I've no idea. They were not in sight, that I remember, when the Truxtons took leave. But I gave them no thought. I've often seen them, and after their exhibition, Mr. Stannard always puts them in his safe himself."

"They have not been found in the safe."

"Then he put them in some simple hiding-place. They will turn up. Unless, of course, there was a real burglar, whose motive was robbery."

"But you do not think so?"

"Frankly, I do not see how there could have been an intruder, unless dressed as a gentleman. No other could have gained access to the house."

"The servants saw no stranger, in any sort of garb?"

"They say so," returned Beatrice, thoughtfully. "Don't overlook the possibility of an accomplice among the servants. I've no reason to think this, but such things have happened."

"They have indeed, and I assure you we have not overlooked the chance of it."

CHAPTER 7: NATALIE, NOT JOYCE

BUT the desired interview with Natalie was not achieved before the funeral of Eric Stannard. It was two days after before the girl would consent to see Roberts, and then, under protest.

"I've nothing to say," she declared, as she came unwillingly into the Reception Room to meet him. "I'm not under arrest, and there's no law that can make me talk if I don't want to."

The lovely face was troubled and the scarlet lips were pouting as Miss Vernon flounced herself into a chair, one foot tucked under her, and one little slipper tapping the carpet. She looked so like a petulant school-girl, it was well nigh impossible to connect her with a thought of anything really wrong. But Robert Roberts was experienced in guile and was by no means ready to accept her innocence at its face value.

"No law ought to make you do anything you don't want to," he said smiling; "but suppose it's to your own advantage to talk?"

The sympathetic, good-natured face of Bobsy Roberts had a pleasant effect, for Natalie's pout disappeared and a look of confidence came into her blue eyes.

"I wonder if I can trust you," she said, meditatively, as she gazed at him, with an alluring intentness.

"You sure can," returned Bobsy, but he consciously and conscientiously steeled himself against her witcheries.

"No, I don't think I can," she said, after a moment, and with a tiny sigh of disappointment, she looked away. "Go on; question me as you like."

"Why can't you trust me?"

"Oh, I trust you, as far as that goes. But I see you suspect me of killing Mr. Stannard."

"And didn't you?" Bobsy believed in the efficacy of sudden, direct questions.

But Miss Vernon was not taken off guard.

"No," she said, quietly, "I didn't. But when I say I didn't, it implicates Mrs. Stannard, and I don't want to do that. Can't you tell me what to do?"

"Well, it's this way. If Mrs. Stannard is the guilty person, you want it known, don't you?"

"No, indeed! If Joyce Stannard killed her husband, she had a good reason for it, and I'd rather nobody'd know she did it."

"What was her good reason?"

"Well, you know, Mr. Stannard was—that is,— he had eyes for other people beside his wife."

"You, for instance."

"Yes!" and the flower face took on a look of positive hatred, and of angry reminiscence. "I have no kindly thought of Eric Stannard, if he is dead."

"He was kind to you."

"Too kind,—in some ways,—and not enough so in others."

"And his wife was jealous?"

"Who wouldn't be! He petted her to death one day and the next he neglected her shamefully. I will trust you, Mr. Roberts. Now, listen; if Joyce killed Eric,—I don't say she did, but if she did, why can't we just hush up the matter, and pry into it no more? Barry wants that and so do I. And who else is to be considered?"

"The law, justice, humanity, all things right and fair."

"Rubbish! Let those things go. Consider the wishes of the people most concerned."

"Then straighten out a few uncertain points. Where are the emeralds?"

"Goodness! I don't know! That foolish letter wasn't written to me."

"To whom, then?"

"I don't know that, either. Some one of Eric's lady friends, I suppose. Fancy my wanting him to divorce his wife and marry me!"

Bobsy looked at her narrowly, distrusting every word. This girl, he felt sure, was far from being as ingenuous as she looked.

"But he was in love with you?"

Natalie blushed, a real, natural girl blush.

"I can't help that, Mr. Roberts. I am, unfortunately, a type that men admire. It is the cross of my life that every one is attracted by my silly doll-face!"

Bobsy Roberts laughed outright, at this naive wail of woe.

"You needn't laugh, I'm in earnest. I get so sick of having men fall in love with me, that I'd like to go and live on a desert island!"

"With whom?" and Bobsy looked at her intently.

"With Barry Stannard," she returned, simply. "We're engaged, now. We couldn't be, while Mr. Stannard lived, for he wouldn't hear of it. Threatened to disinherit Barry, and all that. But now, it's all right."

"Miss Vernon, to my mind, that speech clears you of all suspicion. If you had killed Eric Stannard, because he wouldn't let his son marry you, you never would have referred to it so frankly."

"Of course I wouldn't. Now, don't you see, since I didn't kill him, it must have been Joyce. It's been proved over and over that it could not have been a burglar, or anybody like that. And so, I want to stop investigating, and leave Joyce in peace. And then, after awhile, she can marry Eugene Courtenay, and be happy."

"Does she want to marry Mr. Courtenay?"

"Of course she does. He was in love with her and she with him, before she knew Mr. Stannard. Then Eric came along and stole her,—yes, stole her, —just like a Cave Man. She was carried away by his whirlwind wooing, and—too—he was celebrated, and—well,—you know,—masterful,—and he just took her by storm. She never really loved him, but she has been good and faithful, though he has treated her badly."

"And if she killed him, it was—"

"It was because she had reached the end of her rope, and couldn't stand any more. And, too, she has seen a lot of Mr. Courtenay lately, and—oh, well,—she was mad that Eric took such a fancy to me, and so,"

"Look here, Miss Vernon, just see if you can reconstruct the scene to fit in with a theory of Mrs. Stannard's guilt."

"How do you mean?"

"Can you remember about the light going out and the cry for help,—and all that, exactly?"

"No,—I've tried to, but it's all mixed up in my mind. I think, if Joyce,—I mean, whoever did it, —must have struck the blow, and then turned off the light, and then gone out of the room, and—and come back again."

"And that could have been you—as well as Mrs. Stannard! You were both discovered in practically the same circumstances!"

"You're trying to trip me, Mr. Roberts. But you can't do it. Now, look here, if that note had been written to me, wouldn't it mean that these emeralds were mine, and wouldn't I claim them?"

"But it states distinctly that you know where they are, and the presumption is, that you have them in your possession."

"Indeed, I haven't! I wish I had! I mean, I wish I had them rightfully in my possession! They're wonderful stones! Look here, Mr. Roberts, why don't you suspect Mr. Truxton? He's gem crazy,—and you know gem enthusiasts often go to any length to get the stones they covet."

"I hadn't thought of him. And, supposing he did commit crime to steal Mr. Stannard's jewels, just how did he get away afterward, without discovery?"

"Well, suppose he stabbed Mr. Stannard, then turned off the light, and then slipped out through the Billiard Room when Joyce's back was turned?"

"Too unlikely. Besides, Mr. Courtenay, who sat on the bench on the lawn, just then, would have seen him leave the house."

"I suppose he would." Natalie drew a deep sigh. "Do give it up, Mr. Roberts. You never can untangle it."

"Are you going to stay here long?"

"For a time. Mrs. Stannard has asked me to, and Barry wants me." The simplicity of the girl's manner almost disarmed Bobsy, but he went on:

"Mrs. Stannard, then, has no hard feelings toward you?"

"I don't know. Honestly, Mr. Roberts, I don't know whether she is keeping me here because she suspects me, or because she doesn't."

"Did Mr. Stannard leave you anything in his will?"

The rose-pink cheeks flushed deeper, as Natalie replied, "Yes, he did. You probably know that already."

"No, I didn't. Was it a worthwhile amount?"

"From my point of view, yes. It was seventy thousand dollars."

"Whew! Decidedly worthwhile, from almost anybody's point of view."

"I know what you're thinking," cried Natalie as he paused. "It's an added reason for suspecting me of killing him."

"It might be construed so."

"Well, I didn't! I was pretty mad, when he made that horrid etching from my Goldenrod picture—"

"And you smudged the wax impression so he couldn't use it—"

"I did not! I would willingly have done so, if I'd thought of it, but I didn't do it, all the same."

"Who did?"

"Whoever killed him, I suppose."

"Then that lets out Mr. Truxton, or a burglar of any sort. It leaves only Mrs. Stannard. Mightn't she have done it?"

"A jealous woman might do anything. But Joyce wasn't especially jealous of me,—no more than of anybody Mr. Stannard might be attracted to."

"And to whom else was he attracted?"

"Nobody just now,—that I know of. You see, Mr. Roberts, I was just about to leave this house, because Mr. Stannard was too devoted in his attentions to me. I tell you this frankly, because I want you to understand the situation."

"And I want to understand it. Tell me more of this matter."

"Well, Mr. Stannard had told me several times of his affection for me and had told me he would remember me in his will, and, not more than a week ago, he told me of Joyce's caring for Mr. Courtenay, though how he discovered that, I don't know, for Joyce never showed it. She was good as gold. Well, Mr. Stannard didn't say so in so many words, but he implied that if he and Joyce— separated— and it could be arranged,—and she—you know,— married Mr. Courtenay,—would I marry him. And I was so mad, I flew into a rage, and—"

"And scratched up your picture?"

"No, that wax plate hadn't been drawn then. It was afterward that he drew that, and then I was madder than ever."

"And in the heat of your passionate rage, —"

"No, I didn't! I tell you, whoever killed Eric Stannard, I didn't!"

"Then what did he mean, when, in his dying moment, he said, 'Natalie, not Joyce!' Tell me that—!"

"I will tell you," and the girl lowered her voice and looked very serious. "I know exactly what he meant, and Joyce Stannard knows too. He meant, —you'll think I imagine this, but it's true; he meant that it was Natalie and not Joyce, whom he loved, and whom he was trying to beckon to at that moment."

It was impossible to doubt the honesty of the speaker. The great earnest eyes were filled with mingled pain and shame, but the girl meant what she said.

"I know it," she went on. "You see, he had said to me, several times, 'Natalie, not Joyce,' by way of a teasing bit of love-making. Eric was not a bad man, it was only that he could not keep from making love to any woman he might chance to be with. And when I would reprimand him and bid him go to his wife, he would laugh and say 'Natalie, not Joyce,' till it became a sort of by-word with him. And I know that's what he meant that night, when he was hurt,—he didn't know he was dying,— and he called to me in a half-conscious plea to come to his assistance. Also, he could see me more plainly. Joyce was rather behind him, and his clouding brain spoke out as he saw me, and called for me. As a matter of fact, that speech, though made so much of, means nothing at all. He wasn't entirely conscious and he spoke as one in a dream. But he did not mean that I had stabbed him."

"Did he know who stabbed him?"

"How can I tell that? But if he had known that I did it, or had thought that I did it, he would never have said so, had he been aware of what he was saying."

"You mean, if you had been guilty, he would have shielded you, rather than accused you with his last breath?"

"Yes, or Joyce either. Or any woman. Eric Stannard would never accuse a woman of wrongdoing. His speech meant anything rather than that."

"Miss Vernon, this puts a very different light on your connection with the affair. Why didn't you tell this before?"

"Can't you understand, Mr. Roberts? I have no love for Eric Stannard, I never had any. His attentions annoyed me, his insistence on painting me as he wished to, also annoyed me. I would have left him long ago, but for

Barry. Also, I am fond of Joyce. She has been most kind
to me, and never jealous of me until lately. Now, I hated
to announce that those dying words meant that Mr.
Stannard put me ahead of his wife in his affection,
especially as it didn't altogether mean that, it was merest
chance that he saw me and not her—"

"But he did see her, for he said 'Natalie, not Joyce.'"

"Yes, I know," and the little foot tapped the rug,
impatiently,—"but, I mean, he saw me, and he was for
the moment interested in me, and he was in pain, or a
sort of stupor, or—oh, I don't know what his sensations
were, I'm sure,—but I want to show you that he spoke at
random, and it didn't mean as much as it seems to."

Natalie had grown excited, her lip trembled, and her
voice was unsteady. Either she was desperately anxious
to make the truth clear, or she was making up a
preposterous story.

If she were guilty, this was a great scheme to divert
the suspicion so emphasised by the victim's statement,
and if she were innocent, the story she told might well be
true.

"Let me follow this up," said Bobsy, looking at her
closely. "Then Mr. Stannard was so in love with you that
he called on you in a desperate moment, rather than on
his wife—"

"But he didn't know it was a desperate moment. I
don't believe that man was conscious at all. The stab
wound was practically fatal at once. What he said and did
after it, was involuntary. Don't you know what I mean?
He was only half alive physically and almost not at all
alive in his mind— his brain. Couldn't that be true?"

"I suppose so. In fact, I think it must have been —and
yet, no, it seems to me it would be logical for him to tell,
even without a clear consciousness, who his assailant
was. Remember Blake asked him outright. 'Who did this?'
and he said—"

"I know; but you didn't see him, and I did. He was not
looking at Blake, he didn't even hear him. He was in a

dazed state, and, seeing both Joyce and myself,—he must have seen us both,—his sub-consciousness called out for me. I am not vain of this preference, I wish it had all been otherwise, but I insist that explains his words, and— Joyce knows it, too."

"How do you know she does? Have you talked with her on this subject?"

"Oh, yes. We have discussed it over and over. Mrs. Faulkner and Joyce and Barry and I have gone over every bit of it a dozen times."

"Is it possible? What does each of the four think? Since you deny the deed, you can tell what is the consensus of opinion in the household."

"That's just what I can't do. You see, we all hesitate to say anything that will seem to accuse either of us. Mrs. Faulkner, I can see plainly, is uncertain whether to suspect Joyce or me. She is convinced, of course, that it must have been one of us, but she pretends to think it was a burglar."

"She is fond of you both?"

"Yes, she adores Joyce, and she is most friendly to me. I've only known her since I've been here, but she seems to believe in me, somehow. She understands perfectly, that Mr. Stannard meant just what I say he did, by those words. She knows how he acted toward me, and how Joyce felt about it."

"Then she suspects Mrs. Stannard?"

"She doesn't say so. She sticks to the safe theory of an intruder. You can't blame her. None of us can suspect Joyce. It's too absurd."

"And Barry Stannard, what does he think?"

"Oh, he vows it was an intruder. He's thought up a dozen ways for him to get in and out."

"All equally impossible?"

"I suppose so. Unless,—I hate to say it,—but mightn't Blake have let him out?"

"Not unless it was somebody known to the household."

"Well?" said Natalie Vernon.

CHAPTER 8: THE EMERALDS

YOU mean?" prompted Bobsy.

"Oh, nothing. But,—just supposing, you know. I'm sure I don't want to mention Mr. Truxton or Mr. Wadsworth, but they were both here—"

"Absurd! Why, Mr. Wadsworth was with Mrs. Faulkner in the Drawing Room—"

"Yes, I know. But he came down and went out the door alone, leaving her up there. Now, if he had wanted to, and if he had fixed it up with Blake, couldn't he have gone into the studio, stolen the jewels and killed Eric, and then turned off the light and fled, Blake letting him out the front door?"

"But why would Mr. Wadsworth do that?"

"Why would anybody? I'm only showing you that there are theories that don't include me or Joyce."

"But not tenable theories. Mr. Wadsworth, I've been told, was having a—a romantic tete-a-tete with Mrs. Faulkner."

"Yes, he was asking her, for the 'steenth time, to marry him. But she turned him down again."

"Well, even if she did, probably he didn't give up all hope. And a man, just from a session of that sort, isn't going to commit a crime."

"Oh, well, of course, it wasn't Mr. Wadsworth. But why not consider Mr. Truxton? He's a jewel sharp, too."

"We have considered him. But he and his wife went home earlier—"

"He could have come back, —"

"But he didn't. Miss Vernon, we've gone into all these matters very thoroughly. What do you suppose the Police have been doing? There isn't a possible theory we've overlooked, and it all comes back to the simple facts of the evidence that incriminate either Mrs. Stannard or yourself. I see no reason why I shouldn't tell you this frankly. If you care to say anything further in your own defence, I'd be glad to hear it. Naturally, you hate to accuse Mrs. Stannard, but it rests between you two, and it looks as if an arrest would be made soon."

Bobsy was drawing on his imagination a little, but he was bound to startle some information out of this provoking beauty.

And Natalie was startled. Her face paled as she took in the significance of Roberts' words.

"They won't arrest me, will they?" she whispered in a scared little voice.

"I don't see how they can," and Bobsy looked at the girl, wondering. That child, that little, tender bit of femininity—surely she could never have lifted her hand against a man's life! Even had she wished to, she seemed physically incapable of striking the blow.

"Arrest you! Not much they won't!" and Barry Stannard strode into the room.

Natalie turned to him with a little sigh of relief.

"You won't let them, will you, Barry?" she said, as his arm slipped round her trembling shoulders.

"I should say not! Are you frightening her, Mr. Roberts? You know you've no authority for all this."

"It's my duty to learn all I can. If Miss Vernon is innocent, then Mrs. Stannard is guilty."

"As a choice between the two, it is far more likely to be Mrs. Stannard. But I do not accuse her. I only insist on the impossibility of this child's being a criminal."

"'Course I couldn't," and Natalie smiled at the perplexed Roberts. "And if, to clear myself, I must tell all I know, then I'll tell you that Mrs. Stannard has those emeralds in her possession now."

"She has! How do you know?"

"I passed her room this morning. The door was ajar, and I was about to enter, when I saw her, at her dressing-table, looking over the case of emeralds. I recognised it at once. I've often seen them. I didn't like to intrude, then, so I went on. I thought I wouldn't say anything about it, unless it was necessary."

"It is necessary. Has she had them all the time?"

"Let's ask her," said Barry. "I believe Joyce can explain it."

They sent for Mrs. Stannard, and she came, Mrs. Faulkner accompanying her.

"I found these on my dressing-table this morning," Joyce said, simply, holding out the case of emeralds to the view of all.

"Found them! Where did they come from?" asked Roberts.

"I don't know," and then, seeing the dark looks on the Detective's face, Joyce exclaimed, "You tell about it, Beatrice. I—I can't talk."

"This is the story," said Mrs. Faulkner. "About an hour ago, Mrs. Stannard sent for me to come to her room. I went, and she showed me the case of gems, saying she had found it on her dressing-table when she awoke this morning. It was not there when she retired last night. Further than that, she knows nothing about it."

"You mean, the jewels appeared there mysteriously?"

"Yes. She cannot account for it, herself. We have been talking it over, and it seems to me the only explanation is that one of the servants took them, and then decided to return them. Of course it would be practically impossible for a servant to sell or dispose of them after the publicity that has been given to the matter."

"Of course. But why a servant? Why not a guest—or a member of the household,—or—or Mrs. Stannard, herself?"

"I!" exclaimed Joyce. "Why I've just found them!"

"Didn't you have them all the time?"

"Of course not! How dare you imply such a thing? This morning they were in my room, last night they were not there. They were brought there during the night. It is for you to find out who brought them."

"Was the door of your bedroom locked?"

"No. It is not our habit to lock our doors,—any of us. The outer doors and windows are securely fastened, and we have no reason to distrust any of the servants."

"Where were the gems this morning?"

"On my dressing-table, in my dressing-room, adjoining my sleeping room."

"Who do you think put them there?"

"Whoever stole them the night my husband was killed."

"And who do you think that was?"

"Whoever killed him, of course."

"Perhaps not," said Mrs. Faulkner, thoughtfully. "Perhaps the thief and the murderer were not the same person."

"That may be so," agreed Bobsy. "Have you any theory or suspicion based on the return of the jewels, Mrs. Faulkner?"

"No; except a general idea that the emeralds might have been stolen and returned by a servant, and the murder committed by an intruder."

"Why not assume that the intruder also took the jewels?"

"Only because it would be difficult for him to get into the house and return them to Mrs. Stannard. I can see no explanation of that act save that a servant did it."

"Or an outsider with the connivance of one of the servants."

"Yes, that might be," agreed Mrs. Faulkner. "The mere placing of the case in Mrs. Stannard's dressing-room would not be difficult. The doors all over the house are open or unlocked at night, and a servant could easily slip in and out of the room unheard."

"You heard no unusual sound in the night, Mrs. Stannard?"

"None," said Joyce.

"I'm sorry to disagree with the construction you put upon this incident, Mrs. Faulkner," and Bobsy turned to her as to the principal spokesman, "but to my mind it strengthens the case against Mrs. Stannard. It seems more than likely that she had the emeralds all the time, or knew where they were. She kept them hidden, because she thought the letter written by her husband, tacitly gave the gems to Miss Vernon. Then when Miss Vernon saw her, looking at the jewels, Mrs. Stannard thought better to face the music and own up that she had them."

"Why I didn't let her know that I saw her!" exclaimed Natalie.

"Perhaps she saw you in a mirror, or heard you. Doubtless she knew in some way that you had seen her looking at the jewels, and concluded to tell the story that accounted for them."

Joyce Stannard looked at the speaker, and her face blanched. With a desperate cry of distress, she turned and swiftly left the room. Roberts kept a wary eye on her retreating figure, and as she went upstairs, he made no attempt to recall or to follow her.

"She has practically condemned herself," he said.

"The reappearance of the emeralds seems to settle it."

"Why?" asked Beatrice Faulkner. "Why do you condemn her because of that?"

"Look at it squarely, Mrs. Faulkner. Assume for a moment my theory is right. Then, Mrs. Stannard, being guilty, and wishing to throw suspicion on Miss Vernon, claims that the jewels were put in her room surreptitiously during the night. She is sure Miss Vernon will be suspected of having had the jewels, and, frightened, restored them secretly. This will militate against Miss Vernon, and imply her greater guilt also."

"Why, what an idea!" exclaimed Natalie. "As if I ever had the emeralds!"

"That letter said you knew where they were."

"That letter was not written to me."

"To whom then?"

"I've no idea. But not to me. I'm—I'm engaged to Barry."

"You weren't engaged to the son while the father was alive," probed Roberts.

"N—no. But only because his father wouldn't allow it. I'm going to look after Joyce," and without a backward glance, Natalie ran from the room, and up the stairs.

"You see," began Roberts, looking at Mrs. Faulkner and Barry Stannard, "you two are the only ones

I can talk to frankly. Those two ladies suspected by the police have to be handled carefully. You are both material witnesses, and as such are bound to tell me truthfully all you can of anything bearing on the case. Now, however painful it may be for you, Mr. Stannard, I must tell you that it is rapidly coming to a show-down between the two suspects, and the probability is, it seems to me, that the burden of evidence rests more strongly on the wife than on the model. The direct evidence is perhaps evenly balanced, but it seems to the police that the motive is greater and the opportunity easier for Mrs. Stannard than for Miss Vernon. The wife, let us say, had reason for jealousy, and had reason for wishing to be free of her uncongenial husband. The little model, while irritated at her employer's attentions, was in love with another man, and could easily get away from the artist without resorting to crime."

"That's right about Natalie," exclaimed Barry, "but it's unthinkable that Joyce should go so far as to kill—"

"You don't know all the provocation she may have had," said Roberts. "A jealous wife, or an unloving wife goes through many hard hours before she reaches the point of desperation, but she sometimes gets there, and then the climax comes. At any rate, if Miss Vernon isn't guilty, Mrs. Stannard is. You can't find two women hovering over a dying man, and acquit them both. So it's one or the other, and I incline toward the suspicion of the older woman."

"But how do you explain the various clues pointing to Natalie?" asked Beatrice Faulkner.

"Let's take them one by one. First, that note found on the man's desk. Even if that were written to Miss Vernon, it needn't condemn her. Even if she had been in love with the artist, it is no evidence whatever that she killed him. And the whole tone of the note is against its being meant for her. It is unexplained so far, but I can't look on it as evidence against the model."

"I agree with that," said Mrs. Faulkner. "That letter may well have been to some other woman interested in Eric Stannard, and she may have had the emeralds, and, through connivance with a servant, returned them to Joyce last night."

"No, no, Mrs. Faulkner, that isn't right. I don't understand the emerald business altogether, but I thoroughly believe that Mrs. Stannard has had them in her keeping all the time. Now, next, we have the evidence of the dying man's exclamation. That, I think, is perfectly explained by Miss Vernon's assertion that he meant he loved her and not his wife."

"Of course it is," declared Barry. "I know my father was madly in love with Miss Vernon, and though he was fond of his wife, it was not the first time he had been interested in the pretty face of another woman. I want to say right here, that I revere and respect my father's memory, but I cannot deny his faults. And he was far too careless of his wife's feelings in these matters. My mother died many years ago, and for a long time my father led a butterfly existence, outside of his art, yes, and in it, too. Then when he married a second time he did not settle down to the generally accepted model of a married man, but continued to admire pretty women wherever he met them. Now, it is more than likely that in his dying moments his brain half dazed, and seeing the two before him, he protested his love for the model he admired and put her ahead of his wife. I do not defend my father's speech but to me it is explained."

"It may be so," said Roberts. "Now here's another point. Mrs. Stannard declares she heard her husband talking to another woman or at least to somebody, in his studio, as she herself stood in the Billiard Room, near the connecting door. Shall we say this is an invented story of hers?"

"Let me see," said Barry, "what were the words?"

"To the effect that he was not willing to leave his wife for her, and that as a consolation she could have the emeralds."

"Practically what was in the note," exclaimed Mrs. Faulkner.

"Almost," returned Roberts. "Now was Miss Vernon there and were these words addressed to her? this question being quite apart from consideration of her as the criminal."

"If so, then the letter was to her," said Beatrice.

"And it wasn't," maintained Barry. "My father admired Natalie,—made love to her, we'll say, but he never went so far as to offer her jewels, nor did she want him to marry her, as the overheard conversation implies."

"Could this be the way of it?" said Beatrice. "Suppose Mr. Stannard was even then writing that note—"

"But it was found in his desk."

"Well, suppose he was thinking it over, and muttered to himself the actual wording of it. Mrs. Stannard says she heard no other voice, so may he not have been alone in the studio at that time?"

Bobsy Roberts turned this over in his mind. "It is a possibility," he conceded. "And then, let us say, after hearing those words, Mrs. Stannard entered the room, and confronted him, and perhaps there was a quarrel and in a moment of insane rage,

Mrs. Stannard caught up the etching needle and—"

"It isn't at all like her," said Barry, "but I can only say it is more easily to be conceived of in her case than in Natalie's. I don't want to admit the possibility of Joyce being the criminal, but I can believe it, before I can imagine Natalie doing such a thing. And as you say, Joyce had motive, and Natalie had none."

"I won't subscribe entirely to that, Mr. Stannard. Miss Vernon inherits a goodly sum, and too, she may have been incensed at the manner of the artist toward her—"

"No, I wasn't," said Natalie herself, suddenly reappearing. "On the contrary, I had persuaded Mr. Stannard, that very day, not to ask me to pose for him, except as a fully draped model. He had apologised for his previous insistence, and I looked for no more trouble on that score. I was trying to get up courage to ask him to let Barry be engaged to me, but I hadn't accomplished that."

"If Mrs. Stannard had had any angry words with her husband just before he was attacked, could you have overheard them?" asked Roberts.

"I don't think so. Not unless they had spoken very loudly. The door to the Terrace was closed, or almost closed. And I was not thinking about what might be going on in the house. Unless there had been an especial disturbance, I should not have noticed it."

"Yet you heard that gasping cry for help through the closed door."

"Yes. But that was not a faint gasp, it was a penetrating sort of a cry. An attempted scream, I should describe it."

Roberts looked at her closely. Was she innocent or was she an infant Machiavelli?

"It is a difficult situation," he said, with a sigh. "We have but two eye-witnesses. Each naturally accuses the other and denies her own guilt. One speaks truth and one falsehood. How can we distinguish which one tells the truth?"

"Don't say eye-witnesses," objected Natalie. "I didn't see the crime committed. If I think Joyce did it, it's only because I went in and found her there and nobody else about."

"Suppose," and Bobsy Roberts looked her straight in the face, "suppose Eric Stannard held in his hand your picture,—that etching, you know, and suppose he was, in a way, talking to it. Or, say, he wasn't talking to it, but what he did say, and what his wife overheard, was said while he held your picture, and she thought he referred to you. Then she, in a jealous fury, resented the idea of his giving you the emeralds, and—"

"I didn't want the emeralds," said Natalie, coldly, "and I certainly didn't want Eric to marry me, but even granting your premises right, it takes suspicion of the murder from me, and places it on Joyce."

"It does," agreed Barry, "and that's where it belongs, if on either of you two."

"It must be so," said Beatrice Faulkner, "for if Natalie had known where the emeralds were, and if that letter was written to her, and gave her the gems,—for it really did give them to the one it was written to,—then she would have kept them and not have given them back to Joyce."

"By Jove, that's so!" exclaimed Roberts. "Whatever woman that letter was meant for, is the real owner of the jewels this minute, according to Eric Stannard's wish, and if she had them she would be extremely unlikely to give them up unnecessarily. But how, then, explain their return?"

"It wasn't a return," said Beatrice. "Joyce had them herself all the time."

"I believe she had," said Roberts.

CHAPTER 9: ONE OR THE OTHER

BOBSY ROBERTS was at his wits' end. He pondered long and deeply but he could seem to see nothing to do but ponder. There was no trail to follow, no clue to track down, and no new suspect to consider.

He sat by the hour in the studio, as if he could, by staring about him wring the secret from the four walls that enclosed the mystery.

"Walls have ears," he said to himself, whimsically, "now if they only had eyes and a tongue, they might tell me what I want to know."

The studio furnishings included several small tables and escritoires which had drawers and pigeonholes stuffed with old letters and papers. Like most artists Eric Stannard was of careless habits regarding his belongings. Roberts patiently and laboriously went over these papers, and found little of interest. Old bills, old notes of appointment with patrons, old social invitations and such matters made up the bulk of the findings.

But he came across a small parcel, neatly tied with fine string and looking unmistakably like a jeweller's box. Bobsy opened it, and found a small gold heart-shaped locket. With it was a card bearing the words "For my Goldenheart. From Eric."

It was quite evidently a gift for the one to whom the letter was written, but it had never been presented. It was easily seen that the parcel had been opened, the card put in, and the string retied in the same punctilious fashion that the jeweller had tied it. The paper wrapping was uncrumpled, but it was a little faded by time, and dusty in the creases.

"Bought it for her but never gave it to her," Bobsy surmised. "Surely I can make something out of this."

But nothing seemed definite. A provokingly blank paper, without address of any sort, can't be indicative of much. The box bore the jeweller's name, and possibly a visit to the firm might tell when the trinket was bought, which might mean some help, or, more likely, none.

Bobsy showed it to Joyce Stannard, but she took little interest in it.

"It must have been bought before I married Mr. Stannard," she said.

"Why?"

"I know by the box. That sort of a box was used by that firm the year before I was married. In all probability Mr. Stannard did buy it for a lady, and for some reason or other didn't present it. It's of no great value."

"No," agreed Bobsy, "except as it proves that his interest in 'Goldenheart' has lasted for some time."

"Then Goldenheart can't be Miss Vernon," said Joyce, wearily. "It seems to me, Mr. Roberts, that you get nowhere. You make so much of little things—"

"Because we can't get any big piece of evidence. You know yourself, Mrs. Stannard, that our principal clue is the finding of you and Miss Vernon in a situation which might mean the guilt of either of you, and must mean the guilt of one of you."

"Mr. Roberts, I want to say to you very frankly that I wish to be cleared of suspicion. I did not kill my husband. I can't quite believe Miss Vernon did, but at any rate I want the mystery cleared up. I don't know how to set about it myself, and if you don't either, I want to employ some one else. This is no disparagement of your powers, but if you know of any—more experienced Detective—"

"There are plenty of more experienced detectives, Mrs. Stannard, but I am anxious to succeed in this quest myself. Will you not give me a longer time, and if at the end of, say, another week, I have made little or no progress, call on whomever you like."

"Very well. But I must be freed myself. I am willing to spend a fortune, if need be, but I cannot live under this cloud of suspicion."

"Let us work together then. Tell me anything I ask, and you may be able to give me some help. First, can you state positively that no person came in through the Billiard Room and went on to the studio while you were in the Billiard Room, just before the tragedy?"

"Why, of course, nobody passed through."

"The Billiard Room was lighted?"

"Yes. Not brilliantly, but a few lights were on."

"Mr. Courtenay had just left you?"

"A short time before, yes."

"And,—now think carefully,—could you not have been sitting with your back to the door, or— perhaps, had you your face hidden in your hands, or for any such reason, could some one have passed you without your knowing it?"

Joyce hesitated a moment, and then she said, "No; positively not. I was sitting on one of the side seats, and I may have had my eyes closed, for I was thinking deeply, but if any one had passed through the room I should have heard footsteps, of course."

"On the soft, thick rug?"

"Much of the floor is bare, and my hearing is very acute. Yes, Mr. Roberts, I must have heard the intruder, if one came in that way."

"I do not think one did, but there is no other way for any one to have entered the studio."

"Why not by coming in the Terrace door, and passing Natalie instead of me?"

"The probability is less. The Terrace door was closed, and, too, Miss Vernon sat back on the Terrace, and must have seen any one passing in front of her."

"But suppose she did see him, and chooses to deny it for his sake?"

Bobsy looked at her. "I've been waiting for this," he said. "You mean Barry Stannard. There is room for thought in that direction. He had reason to be angry at his father, first because of his refusal to let Barry marry the girl, and also, because of Eric Stannard's annoyance of the little model. The father out of the way, the son steps into a fortune and wins his bride beside."

"But Barry never did it! I confess I've thought of it as a theory, but I can't believe it of Barry,— I simply can't."

"Mrs. Stannard, somebody killed your husband. If not a common malefactor, who was bent on robbery, then it must have been one of Mr. Stannard's intimates. If that is so, Barry Stannard is no more above suspicion than Miss Vernon or yourself."

"That's true enough. Well, go ahead, Mr. Roberts. Do all you can, but do get somewhere. You reason around in a circle, always coming back to the proposition that it must have been either Miss Vernon or myself."

"That is where I stand at present," said Bobsy, very gravely, "but I shall try to get some new light on it all,— and soon."

Joyce looked after him sadly as he took leave and went away, and as soon as he was gone she threw herself on a couch and cried piteously.

The visit to the jeweller merely corroborated what Joyce had said that the gold heart was bought shortly before her marriage to Eric. The date was looked up and the purchase verified. So it seemed to tell nothing save that it was meant for a gift but never given. Probably, thought Roberts, it was owing to Eric's marriage that he concluded not to give a keepsake to a woman other than his bride. But, after all, mightn't Goldenheart be Joyce herself? No, for the letter found in the desk denied that. But that letter might have been written a long time ago. Not likely, for it stated that Joyce would not be unwilling to consider separation from her husband. That of course, pointed to the fact that Joyce loved another, doubtless Courtenay, but more than all it pointed to Natalie as Goldenheart. Well, it was not inconceivable that Eric Stannard, the gay Lothario, had called more than one woman Goldenheart. Yet had it been Natalie, would he not have said Goldenrod, especially as he had painted her in that guise?

And so, as usual, Bobsy Roberts puzzled round in circles and came back to the old idea that it must be one of those two women, and could not by any possibility be any one else.

And now, to prove it. He planned to delve deeply into the recent past of the two, and also into Eric's behaviour of late, and he felt he must get some hint or some clue to go upon.

Then, too, there were the missing jewels. The emeralds had been returned to Joyce,—that is, she said they had been returned. But the rest of the collection was still unfound. Bobsy didn't think they had been stolen or lost, but merely that Eric had hidden them so securely that they were unfindable. A queer procedure that. It would seem that he would have left some record of their hiding place. But he was a queer man,—careless in every way. And the jewels might be in a bank or Safe Deposit, or might be in some desk or drawer in the house. The whole business was unsatisfactory, nothing tangible to work on. An out and out robbery, now, one might track down. But a jewel disappearance that might be all right and proper, was an aggravating proposition.

So Bobsy Roberts was decidedly disgruntled and not a little chagrined. He had welcomed this great case as an opportunity to show his powers of real detective work. But it was not so easy as he had thought it. It was all very well to say the criminal must be one of two people and quite another thing to bring any real proof, or even evidence, aside from the finding of them present at the scene of the crime.

Bobsy tried to balance up the points against each.

Motive? About equal, for Joyce didn't love her husband, and Natalie was angry at his intentions to her. Inheritance? Equal again, for the seventy thousand dollars that was Natalie's bequest was quite as desirable a fortune for her, as the larger portion that Joyce received was for her. Moreover, Natalie would doubtless marry the son and have a fortune as great as Joyce's. Opportunity? Certainly equal. Both women were alone, within a few steps of the victim, unobserved of anybody, and so familiar with the room and furnishings that they could extinguish the light and still find the way around quietly.

Bobsy visualised the scene. Whichever one did it, after striking the blow, she had to cross the room to the electric light switch by the front hall door, turn it off and then go back again, doubtless meaning to leave the room as she had entered it. But before she had left the room she heard sounds from the wounded man, and paused,—or perhaps she heard the other woman coming in in the darkness, and paused in sheer fright and uncertainty. Then came the sudden, blinding illumination as Blake snapped on the key, and then—discovery by Blake and Mrs. Faulkner both. No escape was possible then. She had to stay and face the issue. Now, which of the two acted the part of guilt? Though not there at the time, Bobsy had had the story repeated by all who were there, and knew it by heart. Natalie had cowered in terror, Joyce had nearly fainted. Surely there was no choice between these as evidence of guilt! Either woman's action was quite compatible with a criminal's sudden action at being discovered, or an innocent woman's horror at the scene before her.

But one had stabbed and one was overcome at the sight. And Bobsy vowed he'd find out which was which before his week was up.

Returning to The Folly, he asked permission to spend some time in Eric's rooms on the second floor. Here he studied his problem afresh. The bedroom, dressing-room and den were all as the dead man had left them. Here again were the untidy cupboards and drawers, for servants had always been forbidden by Eric himself to put his personal belongings in order, and since his death the police had stipulated the same.

But nothing turned up. Sketches, photographs, old letters, all were scanned and perused without throwing one gleam of light on the great question.

Slowly Bobsy walked down stairs, after his fruitless quest. Slowly he went down the great staircase, admiring every inch of the way. He had made rather a study of staircases and this splendid specimen, with its big, square landings interested him greatly. The carved wainscoting, the beautiful newels and balusters were things of beauty and were fully appreciated by the detective. He reached the lower hall and stood thinking of Blake's experience. There the footman had stood, listening at the studio door, when Mrs. Faulkner came down and saw him. Then, in less than a minute they had both entered the studio. No, there was not time for any other intruder to have been in there and to have got away, in the dark, with those two women standing by the dying man. It was a physical impossibility. Now, once again, which?

Joyce passed him as he stood in the hall. Then she turned back and, after a moment's hesitation, she spoke to him.

"Mr. Roberts, I've had a strange letter. I want to ask advice about it. Will you help me?"

"In any way I can, Mrs. Stannard. What is it?"

"Come in the studio. I'll speak to you first about it. I was looking for Barry, to ask him."

They went into the great room, the room about which hung the veil of mystery, and sat down.

"Here is the letter," said Joyce, handing it to him. "I wish you would read it."

Bobsy took the letter curiously. What would he learn?

It was on mediocre paper, and written in a fairly good, though not scholarly looking penmanship. It ran:

Mrs. Stannard:

Dear Madam: Before writing what I am about to reveal, let me assure you that I am in no sense a

professional medium or clairvoyant. I am a woman of
quiet life and simple habits, but I am a psychic, and in a
trance state I have revelations or visions that are
invariably truly prophetic or as truly reminiscent. I
cannot be reached by the general public, but when a case
appeals to me, I communicate with those interested and if
they want to see me, I go to them. If not, there is no harm
done. So, if you are anxious to learn who is responsible for
the death of your late husband, I shall be glad to give you
the benefit of my science and power. If not, simply
disregard this letter.

Very truly yours,
Orienta,

The address was given, and the whole epistle showed
an honest and straightforward air, quite different from
the usual clairvoyant's circular letter.

"It isn't worth the paper it's written on," said Bobsy,
handing it back.

"But how do you know? I've read up on this sort of
thing and while there is lots of fraud practised on a
gullible public, it's always done by a cheap grade of
charlatan, whose trickery is discernible at a glance. This
letter is from a refined, honest woman, and I've a notion
to see what she'll say. It can do no harm, even if it does no
good."

"Of course, Mrs. Stannard, if you choose to look into
this matter I have nothing to say, but you asked me for
advice."

"I know it," and Joyce shook her head, "but if you
don't advise me the way I want you to, I'll—"

"Ask somebody else?"

"Yes, I believe I will."

"Do. I really think if you confer with Barry Stannard
or with Mrs. Faulkner, they would give you advice both
sound and disinterested. They'd probably tell you to let it
alone."

"I'm going to ask them, anyway. I won't ask Natalie, for I don't think she knows anything about it. Why, Mr. Roberts, if we could just get a clue to the mystery, it might be of incalculable help."

"Yes, but you can't get a clue from a fraud."

"I don't believe she is a fraud, but even so, I might learn something from her."

"If you do, I hope you will give me the benefit of the information."

Joyce laid the matter before Barry and Beatrice. Natalie was present also, and Joyce was surprised to find that the girl was well versed in the whole subject of psychics and occult lore.

"I don't know an awful lot about it, Joyce," she said, "but I've read some of the best authorities, and sometimes I've thought I was a little bit psychic myself. I'd like to see this Orienta."

"It doesn't seem right," objected Mrs. Faulkner. "What do you suppose she does? Go into trances?"

"Yes, of course," said Natalie. "And then she talks and tells things and when she comes to again, she doesn't know what she has said."

"Then I don't believe it's true."

"Oh, yes, it is, Mrs. Faulkner. I mean, it's likely to be. Why, if she could tell us who—"

"Do we want her to?" said Barry, very soberly. "Isn't it better to leave the whole thing a mystery?"

"No," said Joyce, decidedly. "I want to find out the truth, if there's any way to do it. I don't think much of detectives, at least, not Mr. Roberts. Oh, he's a nice man,—I like him personally. But he doesn't accomplish anything."

"Well, let's have Orienta come here," suggested Natalie. "And we can see how we like her, and if we don't want her to, she needn't try her powers in our cause."

"The police might object," said Mrs. Faulkner.

"Oh, no," rejoined Barry. "This is a private matter. We're at liberty to do a thing of that sort, if we want to. But I don't approve of it."

"I'm going to write to her, anyway," Joyce declared. "I want to see what she proposes to do."

"Yes, do," urged Natalie. "And ask her to come here as soon as she can arrange to."

CHAPTER 10: ORIENTA

I WISH you'd use your influence with Joyce, and urge her not to have this poppycock business go on." Barry looked troubled, and his round, good-natured face was unsmiling.

"I have tried," returned Beatrice Faulkner, "but she is determined. And, really, it can't do any harm."

"It might turn suspicion in the wrong direction."

"Barry, what are you afraid of? Do you fear any revelation she may make?"

"No, oh, no,—not that. But if—well, supposing she should declare positively that it was Natalie or Joyce,— either of them, don't you see it couldn't help influencing the police? I want the whole thing hushed up. Father is gone, it can't do him any good to find out who killed him, and it may make trouble for an innocent person."

"I'll talk to Joyce again, but I doubt if I can change her determination to ask this Orienta here. Absurd name!"

"Yes, and an absurd performance all round."

"I'll do my best. And, Barry, I'm thinking of leaving here tomorrow; I've stayed longer than I intended, now."

"Oh, don't go away. Why, you're a kind of a —how shall I express it?"

"A go-between?"

"Well, not in the usually accepted sense of that term, but you are that, in a nice way. You can tell Joyce what I can't tell her—at least, what I say to her has no effect. By the way, Joyce wants to go away, too."

"Will they let her?"

"I don't know. But since she is thinking about this Orienta, she's planning to stay here longer. I don't know what she will do, but don't you see, Beatrice, if she goes away, even for a short time, Natalie couldn't stay here without a chaperon? So won't you stay a while longer, until we see how things are going? You've been such a trump all through these troubled days,—why, everybody depends on you to—to look after things, don't you know."

Beatrice smiled at the boy,—for when bothered, Barry looked very boyish,—and said, kindly, "I will stay another week, then. You see, at first, Joyce was so nervous and upset, she asked me to look after the housekeeping a bit, but now her nerves are better, and I think the routine duties of the house help fill up her time, and are really good for her."

"Well, you women settle those matters between yourselves. But you stay on a while, and help me and Natalie through. The girl threatens to go away, too; in fact, everybody wants to get out of this house, and I don't blame them." They were in the studio and Barry looked with a shudder toward the chair where his father had met his death.

"No, I can't blame them either,—and yet, it is a wonderful house. Must it go to strangers?"

"I suppose so. It's Joyce's, of course, but she doesn't want to live here. I don't want to take it off your hands, for Natalie won't live here either. You don't want it, do you?"

"I? Oh, no. My own life here was a happy one, but the memories of those old days and the thoughts of this recent tragedy make the place intolerable to me as a home. But strangers could come in, and start a new life for the old place."

"It isn't old. And it's going to be hard to sell it, because of—of the crime story attached to it. If we could only get matters settled up, and the police off the case, we could close the house and go away. Joyce would go back to her mother's for a time, and eventually, of course, she will marry Courtenay. He's a good chap, and there's not a slur to be cast on him. As long as my father lived, Eugene never said a word to Joyce that all the world mightn't hear."

"How do you know?"

"I only assert it, because I know the man."

"Barry, you're very young, even younger than your years. Try to realise that I'm not saying a word against Joyce or Mr. Courtenay, either, but —well, since your father himself realised how matters stood between them, you ought to see it, too."

"I know they cared for each other, but I mean, Joyce and Eugene both were too high-minded to let their caring go very far."

"High-mindedness is apt to break through when people skate on thin ice. But don't misunderstand me. Keep your faith in all the high ideals you can, both in yourself and others. What did you think of your father leaving such an enormous sum to Natalie?"

"It was more than I supposed, but father was absurdly generous, and often in erratic ways. He probably made that bequest one day when he was especially pleased with her posing, or, more likely, when he himself had worked with special inspiration and had produced a masterpiece."

"Very likely. Miss Vernon doesn't seem surprised about it."

"Oh, she knew it. He told her a short time ago."

"Do the police know that?"

"I fear so. And those are the things that worry me. If they think Natalie killed my father to get that money, it is a strong point against her. Of course, she didn't, but all the evidence and clues in this whole business are misleading. I never saw or heard of such a mass of contradictory and really false appearances. That's why I'd rather hush it all up, and not try to go farther."

"Here comes Natalie now. I'll leave you two alone and I'll go to see what I can do with Joyce about that clairvoyant matter."

Barry scarcely heard the last words, for the mere sight of Natalie entering the room was enough to drive every other thought from his mind. Her white house gown was of soft crepe material, with a draped sash of gold silk, a few shades deeper than her wonderful hair. Gold-hued slippers and stockings completed the simple costume, and in it Natalie looked like a princess. With all her dainty grace and delicate lines, the girl had dignity and poise, and as she walked across the room Barry thought he had never seen anything so lovely.

"You angel!" he whispered; "you gold angel from a Fra Angelico picture! Natalie, my little angel girl!"

He held out his arms, and the girl went to him, and laid her tiny snowflake of a hand on his shoulder.

"Why do you stay in this room, Barry? I don't like it in here."

"Then we won't stay. Let us go out on the Terrace in the sunlight."

The Autumn afternoon sun was yet high enough to take the chill off the crisp air, and on a wicker couch, covered with a fur rug, they sat down.

"Here's where we sat, the night of "began Barry, and then stopped, not wanting to stir up awful memories.

"I know it," returned Natalie. "You left me here,— where did you go, Barry?"

"Off with Thor and Woden for a short tramp. You said you were going upstairs, don't you remember?"

"Yes. But where did you tramp?"

"Oh, around the grounds."

"Which way?"

"What a little inquisitor! Well, let me see. We went across this lawn first."

"Did you see Mr. Courtenay on that stone bench there?"

"No, I don't think so. No, I'm sure I didn't. Why?"

"I just wanted to know. Where did you go next? Come, Barry, I'll go with you. Go over the same path you went that night."

Barry looked at her curiously, and said, "Come on, then."

They started across the lawn, and soon Natalie turned and looked back. "Could you see me from here?" she asked.

"Not at night, no. But I didn't try. I thought you had gone in the house, and I went straight ahead. The dogs were jumping all over me, and I was thinking of them."

"Oh, Barry! After the conversation we had just had, were you thinking of the dogs instead of me?"

"Well, the dogs were bothering me,—and you weren't I—"

"Where next?"

But Barry hesitated. "By Jove. I don't know which way I did go next. Let me see."

Natalie waited. "Down to the Italian gardens?" she said at last.

"No,—that is, I don't think so. Where did I go?"

"Barry! You must know where you went. How silly."

"It isn't silly. I—I can't remember,—that's all."

"Then you refuse to tell me?"

"I don't refuse,—I just don't remember."

"Barry! Do remember. You must!"

After a moment's silence, he turned and met her gaze squarely, saying, "I have no recollection. Don't ask me that again."

Natalie gave him a pained, despairing look and without a word, turned their footsteps toward the Italian gardens, the beautiful landscape planned and laid out by a genius. Down the stone steps they went and paused in the shadow of a clump of carved box. Then Barry took her in his arms. "Dear little girl," he breathed in her ear, "don't be afraid. It will all come out right. But we don't want the truth known. Now, don't give way," as a sob shook Natalie's quivering shoulders. "You mustn't talk or think another word about it. Obey me, now, take your mind right off the subject! Think of something pleasanter,—think of me!"

"I can't very well help that,—when you're so close!" and the lovely deep blue eyes smiled through unshed tears.

"You heavenly thing! Natalie, have you any idea how beautiful you are?"

"If I am, I am glad, for your sake. I needn't ever pose again, need I, Barry?"

"Well, I guess No! A photograph of you, all bundled up in furs, is the nearest I shall ever let you come to a portrait! Dear, when will you marry me?"

"Oh, I can't marry you! I can't—I can't!"

"Then what are you doing here? This is no place for a girl who isn't to be my wife!" and Barry caressed with his fingertips the pink cheek which was all of the flower-face that showed from the collar of his tweed jacket.

"I oughtn't to be here—but—but I love you, Barry, I do—I do!"

"Of course you do, my blessed infant. Now, as we didn't get along very well with our marriage settlement for a topic, let's try again. Beatrice wants to go away from here. Do you want her to?"

"Oh, no! Don't let her go. I'd be lost without her. I want to go, you know, but I can't, I suppose. Beg her to stay as long as I do,—won't you, dear?"

The pleading in the blue eyes was so tender and sweet that Barry kissed them both before replying. "I will, darling. I'll beg anybody in the world for anything you want, if I have to become a professional mendicant. Now, brace up, Sweetheart, for I want to talk to you about lots of things, and how can I, if you burst into tears at every new subject I bring up?"

"I'm upset to-day, Barry mine. Don't let's talk. Just wander around the gardens."

"Wander it is," and Barry started off obediently, still with his arm round her.

"Unhand me, villain," she said, trying to speak gaily. But it was impossible, and the scarlet lips trembled into a curve that broke Barry's heart for its sadness. He gathered her to himself.

"Dear heart, you are all unstrung. Go to your room for a time, don't you want to? Let Beatrice look after you,—she's kindness itself."

"Indeed she is. I'll do that. And I'll come back, Barry, a new woman."

"For heaven's sake, don't do that! You'd make a fine militant suffragist I—"

"No, not that. But a sensible, commonplace girl, who can talk without crying."

"Commonplace isn't exactly the word I'd choose to describe you, you wonder-thing! But run away and powder your nose, it needs it. Ha, I thought that would stir you up!" as Natalie pouted. "Run along, and I'll see you at dinner time. And this evening we'll have our chat."

But that evening Orienta came. Joyce had refused to listen to any one's objections and had made the appointment with the clairvoyant to come for a preliminary conference whether she gave them a seance or not.

Barry and Natalie refused at first to meet the visitor, but Joyce persuaded them to see her, so that they might argue intelligently for or against her. Beatrice consented to be present, for Joyce had begged it as a special favour.

And so, when Blake ushered the stranger into the Reception Room she was greeted pleasantly by all the members of the household.

Nor was this perfunctory, for the charm of the guest was manifest from the first. At her entrance, at the first sound of her low, silvery voice, each hearer was thrilled as by an unexpected bit of music

"Mrs. Stannard?" she said, as Joyce rose and held out her hand. The long cloak of deep pansycoloured satin fell back showing its lining of pale violet, and the dark Oriental face lighted with responsive cordiality, while she returned the greetings.

Selecting a stately, tall-backed chair, Orienta sank into it, and crossed her dainty feet on a cushion which Barry offered. Her purple hat was like a turban, but its soft folds were neither conspicuous nor eccentric. She chose to keep her hat on, and also retained her long cloak, which, thrown back, disclosed her robe of voluminous folds of dull white silk. Made in Oriental design, it was yet modishly effective and suited well the type of its wearer.

Though not beautiful, the woman was wonderfully charming. In looking at her each auditor forgot self and others in contemplation of this strange personality. Each of the four observing her had eyes only for her, and didn't even glance aside to question the others' approval.

Without seeming to notice this mute tribute, Orienta began to speak. "We will waste no time in commonplaces," she said, her voice as perfectly modulated as that of a great actress, "they cannot interest us at this time. It is for you to tell me whether or not you wish to command my services in this matter of mystery. If so, well,—if not, I go away, and that is all."

The name she had chosen to adopt was a perfect description of her whole personality. Her oval face was of olive complexion; her eyes, not black, but the darkest seal brown; her hair, as it strayed carelessly from the edges of the confining turban, was brown, in moist tendrils at the temples, as if she were under some mental excitement.

It was evident,—to the women, at least,—that the scarlet of her full lips, and the flush on her cheek bones, was artificial, but it gave the impression of being frankly so, and not with intent to deceive. It was perfectly applied, at any rate, and the flash of her ivory white teeth made her smile fascinating.

"That's the word," Barry Stannard thought, as it occurred to him, "she's fascinating, that's what she is. Not entirely wholesome, not altogether to be trusted, but very, very fascinating."

With a subtle understanding, Orienta perceived that Barry had set his stamp of approval on her, and turned her attention to the women.

"I in no way urge or insist upon my suggestions," she said. "I only tell you what I can do, and it is for you to say. For you, I suppose, Mrs. Stannard?"

"Yes," said Joyce, and her tone was decided. "Yes, it is for me to say, and I say I want you. I want you to tell us anything you can,—anything— about the mystery that has come to this house. I want to know who killed my husband, and I want to know why, and all the details of the deed."

"Oh," Barry protested, "don't begin with that, Joyce. Let Madame Orienta tell us something of less importance first. Let us have a seance or a reading or whatever the proper term may be, and test her powers."

The visitor gave him a slow smile. "It is as I am instructed," she said, in a matter-of-fact, every-day sort of way. But I must inform you before going further, that my fees are not small. Test my powers in any way you choose, but I must include the test in my final statement of your indebtedness."

"All right," said Barry. "I'll pay the test bill, and then, Joyce, if you want to go on with your plans, you can assume the further expense."

"Can we do anything to-night?" asked Natalie. She had sat breathless, listening, but now, with eyes like stars, she eagerly questioned.

"You are interested?" and Orienta looked at her.

"Oh, so much. But I fear what you will reveal—"

"Fear my revelations I—"

"Only because I know they will not be true, but you will make us think they are."

Instead of being annoyed or offended, Orienta looked at her and smiled from beneath her heavy dark brows. "You are psychic, yourself," she said.

"Yes," said Natalie, "I am."

CHAPTER 11: SEALED ENVELOPES

WITH a high hand Joyce carried the matter through. She ignored opposition and met remonstrance with a baffling disdain. She arranged for a return of Orienta for the experiments on the following evening, and after the departure of the medium, she declared she would listen to no comments on her actions and went off at once to her own rooms.

Beatrice Faulkner expressed herself guardedly. "I don't care what revelations come," she said, "except as they affect you people here. It doesn't seem to me that that woman can say anything to make me think either Joyce or Natalie committed the crime, but I don't want her to say anything that will make either of them uncomfortable."

"She won't promise that," said Beatrice. "Joyce is bound to see it through. I don't know what she expects from it, but she has no fear, that's certain."

Orienta had stipulated that the seance take place in the studio, saying that the influences of the place would go far toward producing favourable conditions for her.

So they awaited her there, at the appointed time, and within a few minutes of the hour she arrived. Pausing in the hall to lay off her wraps, Orienta then glided into the great room where her group of auditors were assembled. This time she wore a robe of dark green, as full and flowing as the white one. There was no suggestion of Greek drapery, but an Oriental style of billowing folds that would have been hard to imitate. A jade bracelet showed beneath the flowing sleeve and a jade ring was on one finger of the long, psychic hand.

"May I look at it?" said Natalie, as they sat a moment, before beginning the seance.

"Certainly. It is my talisman,—my charm. Without it, I could do nothing."

"Really? How wonderful!" and the girl looked earnestly at the carven stone. "Your power is occult, then?"

"I think it must be. Yet I would not be classed with the people who go by the general title of mediums. They are, usually, frauds."

Orienta made this statement simply, as if speaking of some matter unconnected with her own work or claims. She gave the impression that if fraudulent "mediums" wished to impose upon the gullible public, it was of no interest to her, but she declined to be considered one of them. And so secure was she in her own sincerity, she deemed it unnecessary to emphasise or insist upon it.

"What is your wish?" she asked, at length. "Will you try me first on some outside matters or shall we proceed at once to the question of the mystery we seek to solve?"

Just then Robert Roberts was announced.

"What shall we do?" exclaimed Natalie. "Tell him to come some other time?"

"No," said Joyce, "let him come in here with us. You don't mind, do you, Madame Orienta?"

"No; why should I? Who is he?"

"The detective who is working on the case."

Orienta shrugged her shoulders. "Of course it matters not to me. But are you sure you want him to know what I may reveal? It may incriminate—"

"I don't care who may be incriminated!" exclaimed Joyce. "I want to find out a few things. As a matter of fact, I asked Mr. Roberts to come."

Natalie turned pale. Had Joyce laid a trap? And for whom? What might they not learn before the evening was over?

Bobsy entered, and was duly presented to the visitor. He was courteous, but unmistakably curious.

"What may I call you?" he asked, as he bowed before her.

"Priestess, if you please," she returned. "I refuse to be called a medium or a seeress or even a clairvoyant. I am these things, but the titles have been so misused that I claim only to be a Priestess of the Occult. This is no academic title, I simply name myself a priestess of the cult I express and follow."

"Priestess, I greet you," said Bobsy, and to those who knew him a shade of mockery might be detected in his tone. But it was the merest hint and quite unobservable to the one he addressed. In most decorous manner he took a place in the group, and Joyce announced the plan she had in mind.

"First," she said, "we will have an exhibition of Orienta's powers. We will follow her instructions and she will give us a showing of her methods and her feats. Then,—if I say so,—we will proceed to try the other experiment."

"It is well," said the Priestess. "Remember, please, I make no claims to magic or to witchcraft. I have, within myself, some inexplicable, some mysterious power that enables me to see clairvoyantly through material substances. I have also an occult power which allows me to see happenings at a distance or in the past as if they were transpiring here and now. These two powers are at your disposal, but further than that I cannot go. I cannot answer questions, unless they come within the range of the two conditions I have mentioned to you just now. I cannot read the future or tell fortunes. I can only see what is shown to me, and if I disappoint you, I cannot help it. Now let us proceed. I will ask you each to write a question on a slip of paper and enclose it in an envelope. Sign your name to your question and seal the envelope securely."

"Old stuff," said Bobsy Roberts to Barry, in a low whisper. But Barry shook his head. He would not commit himself until the experiment was over.

"Will you get some paper and envelopes?" asked Orienta. "Any sort will do."

Barry rose and went to the desk nearest to him. There was a small paper pad, and in a pigeon-hole were several small envelopes.

"Will these do?" he asked.

"Any kind will do," said Orienta, wearily, rather than petulantly.

Bobsy looked at her closely. Surely she wasn't at all particular about the materials used. He must watch carefully for hocus pocus, if he was to discover any.

"Ink or pencil?" said Barry.

"It doesn't matter," and Orienta was almost irritated now. "I'm not doing legerdemain tricks, with prepared paraphernalia!"

Barry, a little embarrassed, picked up a pencil, but in trying it, broke off its point. So he took ink, and wrote on the top slip of the pad a short question. This he tore off and passed the pad to Joyce.

At last, each had written a question, signed the slip, tucked it in an envelope and sealed the envelope. Also each put a small private mark on the outside of his or her envelope to distinguish it again.

"Collect them, Mr. Roberts, please," said Orienta, with a gentle smile.

Bobsy put the five envelopes in a little pack and held them.

"Now," said Orienta, "I propose to read these questions in the dark and without opening the envelopes. It is no trick, as you can readily see for yourselves, but I must ask you to sit quietly and not ask questions until I have finished. Then ask whatever you choose. If you please, Mr. Roberts, hand me the envelopes, and then turn off the lights. Or, stay, turn off the lights first, that there may be no chance of my seeing even a mark on the outside."

Bobsy did exactly as directed. Orienta sat in a large chair, facing the others, who sat in a row before her. The lights were arranged so that Bobsy might turn off all at the main switch, save one small table light, which would give him opportunity to regain his seat, and then this could be also turned off.

With everybody raptly watching, Roberts, holding the envelopes, turned off the lights. The room was dark, save for the one shaded lamp glowing on a small table. Then he handed the lot of sealed envelopes to Orienta, who took them in a handclasp that precluded her seeing any detail of them. In another second, Bobsy had taken his seat, and snapped off the last small light. The room was in perfect darkness. Barry's hand stole out and clasped Natalie's, but otherwise there was no movement on the part of any one.

Not a second seemed to have passed before Orienta's soft voice was heard.

"I will read the questions," she said, "in the order they were given me. This is the first: 'Who is Goldenheart?' It is signed Joyce Stannard. This is the answer, as my mind sees it. A woman sitting on a rocky seat near a rushing brook or river. There is a man near her. He bends above her, and speaks endearing words. He calls her Marie, she calls him Eric. She is small and pale. Her hair is Titian red. Though not beautiful, she is attractive in a pathetic way. Ah, the vision is gone."

As the low voice ceased, there was a slight rustle as of some one about to speak.

"No questions, please," said Orienta, "unless you want this experiment to stop right here. I will now read the contents of the next envelope. This is, 'Who marred my etched picture?' signed Natalie Vernon. My mind sees the artist who made it, himself scratching it. He is in a fury. It is because he does not feel satisfied with his own work. He mutters, 'Not right I no, not right, yet!' There is no one with him. He is alone. The vision fades."

Orienta paused, and gave a little soft sigh, as if exhausted. But in a moment she spoke again. "You know," she said, "if you prefer to have the lights, it doesn't matter at all to me. I read these in the dark because I think if the room were lighted you might suppose I saw the message in some way by means of my physical eyes. It is not so, but if you prefer the light, turn it on."

"I do," cried Roberts, and before any one could object, he snapped on the table light and then the main key which flooded the big room with illumination.

Orienta smiled. "I thought you were sceptical, Mr. Roberts," she said. And then, as if his doubts were of little consequence, she said, "Shall I proceed?"

Joyce nodded, but she shot a gleam of annoyance and reproof at Bobsy Roberts, who looked a little crestfallen, but determined to take no chances.

Orienta picked up the next envelope. She had laid aside on a table the two she had read.

She did not look at the envelope she now held, but looked straight at Roberts, as if to convince him of her honesty.

"This is signed Beatrice Faulkner, and it says, 'Where are the lost jewels?' My mind sees this picture. The jewels, not lost, but safely hidden. They are in a strong box, not a safe, more like a metal-bound trunk. I cannot tell where this box is, but it is in a bare place, like a store room or safety place of some sort. The vision goes."

"May we speak?" asked Natalie, eagerly.

"Not yet, please," and the Priestess smiled at her. "May I not have my conditions complied with?"

"Keep still, Natalie," said Barry. "Let her have fair play."

"This is Mr. Stannard's question," and Orienta held another envelope in her long fingers, "'Would it not be wiser not to attempt to solve the mystery, but to hush up the whole matter?' My mind sees a picture. It is vague, there is no detail, but it is bright and beautiful. There are fair flowers and soft colours. They shift, like a kaleidoscope, but always rosy and lovely. It means, yes, it would be better to give up trying to solve the riddle."

"And now," Orienta spoke in a distinctly scornful voice, "there is but one more, Mr. Roberts' envelope. In it he has written, 'Are you a fraud?' I answer this as carefully as I do the others. My mind shows me myself, and I see my honest attempts to do my duty and to read aright. No, I am not a fraud. That is all."

"For shame, Mr. Roberts!" cried Joyce, angrily. "I am sorry I asked you here to-night, and I will now ask that you go away. I am more than interested in Orienta's work, I am enthralled, and I refuse to have it interrupted or interfered with by your unjust suspicions and rude behaviour! Please go away, and let us continue our experiments in peace."

"Oh, Mrs. Stannard, please let me stay," begged the penitent Bobsy; "I'll be good, I promise you. You see, I'm so interested in the thing, I wrote that to test it, and Madame Orienta came through with flying colours. If you will let me remain, I promise not to offend again, in any particular."

Bobsy had a way with him, and Orienta herself smiled a little as she said, "Let him stay. I'm glad to convince him."

So Bobsy staid.

Then Barry proposed that they try the same test over again, but without signing their papers. "Thus," he said, "we will feel more free to ask what we choose."

Orienta agreed, and again each wrote a question, and sealed it in an envelope.

"Seal them with wax, if you wish," said the Priestess, smiling at Bobsy. "I see there is a sealing set right there on the desk."

So Bobsy and Natalie sealed their envelopes, and stamped them with their rings.

"I won't do that," said Joyce, "it's too silly. We all know there's no trick in it."

"Shall I read these in the dark or in the light?" asked Orienta, as Bobsy held the five missives toward her.

"Why not as you did before?" said Beatrice, "part of them in darkness and part in light. I think those read in the dark even more wonderful than in the light."

"So do I," agreed Joyce. "But we'll try both ways. Which first?"

"You may choose," said the Priestess.

"Dark, then," replied Joyce.

So again the room was made totally dark, and immediately came Orienta's soft, velvety tones.

"'Will what I fear ever happen?'" she read slowly. Then she sighed, "I cannot say, my child." Every one present knew she spoke to Natalie, although the question had not been signed. "I hope not,—I think not,—but the vision is clouded. It is better that you forget all. Forget the past, live for a bright and happy future. The vision fades."

They had come to know that that last phrase meant the end of a subject, and the next one would ensue.

With scarcely a pause and without hesitation, Orienta went on:

"'What can I do to help?'" No hint was needed, for all felt sure this was Beatrice Faulkner's question.

The Priestess spoke impersonally, in even tones,and said: "Nothing more than you are doing. Your kindness, cheer and sympathy are needed here and they are appreciated."

"The rest in the light?" asked Bobsy Roberts, impatiently.

"If you choose," returned Joyce, and Roberts switched on the electrics.

Orienta, with closed eyes, sat holding the next envelope in readiness. She seemed not to know or care whether it was light or dark.

"'Am I doing right?' " she read. For an instant the long lashes on the cheeks of the Priestess lifted, and she flashed a momentary glance at Joyce. "Yes, you are doing right. Continue in the procedure you have planned."

A look of contentment passed over Joyce's face. She showed intense relief, and oblivious to the others' curious glances she drew a long sigh and relaxed in her chair.

Clearly, it made no difference to Orienta that the questions were not signed. She knew at once who wrote each. Next came Barry's.

Still with her eyes closed, she held it out toward him, and read, "'Will the truth ever be known?'"

There was a perceptible pause before she said, "You do not want it known, because you fear it. But your secret is safe. That, at least, will never be known."

Bobsy Roberts listened attentively. So Barry Stannard had a secret. Pshaw! Not necessarily because this faker said so! And yet, was she a faker? Bobsy looked at her. He himself had put those sealed envelopes into that long, inert hand. There they were still, intact, seals unbroken, and the reader paying no more attention to them than as if they were so much blank paper. Whatever her power, it was superhuman. No physical vision could read through those opaque envelopes, or if such sight might be, it could not operate in total darkness. No, there was no chance for trickery. It was a supernatural gift of some sort.

His own envelope came last. He had boldly written, "Who killed Eric Stannard?" a question no one else had felt like putting down in crude words.

Orienta read it, her hand clasped over the envelope and her eyes closed.

"At last," she murmured, in a strained, whispering voice, "at last we come to the vital question. It matters not who wrote it, it is what each one wanted to write. Shall I answer?"

There was silence.

Orienta opened her eyes and cast a slow glance around. "I feel as you do, and I want to try her on any ordinary subject first—"

"But we are going to do that," put in Natalie. "I'm crazy to see the whole performance, but I'm scared, too. I wish Joyce would promise not to go on with it if any one of us doesn't like it."

CHAPTER 12: A VISION

IT was curious to note the various expressions that met the eyes of the Priestess.

Bobsy Roberts regarded her with awe. All his scepticism was gone; he was ready to believe anything she might say. She had stood the severest tests, had tossed them aside without noticing them, and had come triumphant through the experimental ordeal. Surely, if she revealed anything hitherto unknown, it would be the truth. But could she do that?

Natalie and Barry both showed fear. Strive to hide it as they would, it lurked in their staring eyes, it was evident in their restless hands, and as if moved by the same thought, they turned and gazed at each other.

Beatrice Faulkner looked troubled. She saw the two young people in their distress, and she looked at the Detective furtively.

Joyce, however, was the one to whom all turned, breathlessly awaiting her decision.

"Yes," she said, and her voice rang out with its note of determination, "yes, Madame Orienta, tell all you know,—all you can learn by your mystic power."

As if in obedience to a command, the graceful figure of the Mystic fell, into a languid pose. Her arms fell limply, her head drooped a very little to one side. Her eyes were open, but seemed to be unseeing, for her glance was fixed, as if watching a mirage.

She looked directly toward the chair where Stannard had died. Her half-vacant glance centred on it, and in a moment she began speaking. She sounded as one in a trance. She was alive but not alert, like one sleep-walking or talking in a dream.

"I see it all,—clearly. I see the artist in his favourite chair. He is at his work,—no, not working, but gazing at something, criticising work that he has done. It is not a picture—it is a small panel. He takes up a tool,—an instrument, a sharp, pointed one. He hesitates, and then with a sudden angry exclamation, he scratches and mars the work. It pleases him that he has done so, and he smiles. A man enters."

There was a stir among her audience. The tension was too great. Barry sought Natalie's hand and clasped it tightly. Roberts shot glances quickly from one to another, but returned his gaze at once to the speaker. Joyce and Beatrice leaned forward, fairly hanging on the words of revelation.

"The man,—he is big and dark,—confronts the artist as he sits. The intruder, without a word, grasps the sharp tool from the fingers of the one who holds it, and thrusts it into the breast of his victim. He darts across the room, turns off all light, and—it is so black,—I cannot see him depart. But—I hear him—I hear his stealthy tread. He comes back, past the dying man,—he hears a groan,—he pauses,—I can see nothing, but I hear two come in at opposite doors. They stand, breathing heavily in fear—in horror of—they know not what. As they stand, half-dazed—I hear the man —the murderer slip past one of them, and out of the room. The light flashes on. The room is dazzlingly bright. I see the two who first entered. They are women. They gaze affrightedly at each other and then at the man in the chair. Two others have appeared. They are at the other end of the long room. It must have been one of these who flashed the light on. They are a man,—a servant he is,— and a woman. Both are terrorised at what they see. The two women near the chair of the dying man accuse each other of the crime. But this is the frenzied cry of shock and fright. They do not mean it— they scarce know what they utter. The dying man raises his head in a final effort of life. He sees the scene with the clearness of the dying brain. He hears the servant say, 'Who did this?'

He replies, with upraised, shaking finger—'Natalie — nor Joyce.' He means neither of these innocent women was concerned. He tries to tell more, to tell of his assailant, but Death claims him. His voice ceases, his heart stops beating,—he is gone. That is all. With his last breath he tried to say, 'Neither Natalie nor Joyce,' but his failing speech rendered the words unintelligible. The vision fades."

Orienta ceased speaking, her eyes drooped shut and she lay back in her chair as one asleep.

The silence remained unbroken for a minute or more. The beautiful voice still rang in their ears. They were still back in the scene they had heard described. The vividly drawn picture was still with them, and there was no reaction until Bobsy Roberts said, in a tone of awed belief, "By Jove!"

Then the stunned figures moved. Beatrice looked at Joyce with a smile of deep thankfulness, and then turned to smile at Natalie. The girl was radiant. She had sensed acutely the whole scene, and she realised perfectly what the revelation meant. Barry was looking at her adoringly, and his face was full of triumphant joy.

Joyce looked still a bit dazed. Had the experiment really proved so much more successful than she had dared to hope? She looked at Roberts. He was scribbling fast in a notebook, lest some point of the story escape his memory.

Orienta opened her eyes, roused her long, exquisite figure to an upright posture, and passed her hand gently across her brow.

"Is it enough?" she asked. "'Are you satisfied?"

"May we ask questions?" eagerly exclaimed Bobsy.

"Yes, but only important ones. I am very weary."

"Then please describe more fully the man who struck the blow."

Again Orienta's eyes fastened themselves on the big armchair.

"I see him clearly," she said, clasping her hands in her tense concentration, "but his back is toward me as he bends over his victim."

"How is he dressed?"

"I cannot quite tell. His figure is vague. His clothes seem merely a dark shadow against the light."

"Does it seem to be evening dress?"

"It may be. I cannot say, surely."

"At any rate, it is not the rough dress of a tramp or burglar?"

"No,—not that, I think."

"He is not masked?"

"No."

"You say he is dark? Pardon me, Madame, but it is my duty to get these details."

"Yes, his hair, as I see it, is dark."

"And he has a round, smooth-shaven face?" Roberts spoke eagerly, as if he had in mind a distinct personality.

"No," said Orienta slowly. "No, he has a long, thin face—"

"Can you see his face, then?" Bobsy fairly shot out the words.

"Not his face, but an indication of his profile—"

"Then is he clean-shaven?"

"No, he wears a beard."

"Oh. A dark beard? A heavy one?"

"Dark, yes. But not heavy."

"Pointed or full?"

"Somewhat pointed—ah, he has turned away. I cannot tell."

"Is he wearing a hat? But, no, you see his hair."

"I see no hat."

"Is there a hat on the table? On a chair?"

"I cannot tell. The vision fades."

"Let up, Roberts," said Barry. "We are sure now the man was an intruder. Let it go at that. If you can find such a one, it won't matter whether he had a hat or not."

"It is important," insisted Bobsy. "Now, Madame Orienta, tell us again of his actions. Even if the vision has faded, tell from your memory what he did. You saw him when he crossed the room toward the hall door. It was light then?"

"Yes. He moved swiftly, straight to the electric switch, and pressed it. Then I could see no more."

"Of course not. But you heard his steps returning, you said."

"Yes, he went stealthily, but I heard him feel his way by the furniture and walls."

"And at the same time you heard a sound from Mr. Stannard?"

"Yes, a sort of gasp or groan."

"Right. It was this, then, that attracted the attention of Mrs. Stannard and Miss Vernon, and they entered at about the same time?"

"So far as I can judge. They were both there when the lights re-appeared."

"And in that brief instant the man had slipped past one of them and escaped."

"That is as the vision revealed it."

"Only one more question. Past which woman did he go?"

"I cannot say. I merely heard a quick footstep at that end of the room."

"It couldn't have been past Miss Vernon," said Bobsy. "She was too near the door, according to her own account. And I don't see how he could have passed Mrs. Stannard, as there was a low light in the Billiard Room, and she must have seen him pass."

"Both women were looking toward the source of the sound they heard. Also, at that very moment, the wounded man gave a faint cry of 'Help!' An instant after, the servant turned on the light. In that instant the man disappeared, unnoticed by any one. I am not explaining these occurrences, Mr. Roberts; I am describing them. It is for you to interpret their meaning."

Bobsy fell into a brown study, and timidly Natalie put forth a question.

"How do you know he said, or tried to say, 'Neither Joyce nor Natalie'?"

Orienta looked at the girl with an affectionate expression.

"You are a 'sensitive' yourself, Miss Vernon. It will not be difficult for you to understand. By my clairvoyance I read the thought in his mind. I know he feared one or other of the two women he saw might be suspected. The dying often have abnormally acute prescience. To ward off any such danger, and in reply to the servant's inquiry, he strove to say neither of you were implicated,—he raised his hand in protest,—but he was physically unable to articulate clearly, and so his words were misconstrued."

"You heard the words," said Natalie to Beatrice Faulkner; "does it seem to you he meant that?"

"Yes," was the reply. "Now that I think it over I feel sure he did. At the moment, you know, I could scarcely control my senses, and his voice sounded so queer and unnatural, it was difficult to gather his meaning."

"I think so, too," broke in Joyce. "I know that's what he meant. Eric's very nature was against his accusing any woman of wrong-doing. He meant just what Madame Orienta has told us. And I am glad there can be no more doubt about it."

"Could a man have brushed by you that moment, Mrs. Stannard?" asked Bobsy.

"I suppose so. I came from a lighted room into one of pitch blackness. I heard a quick breathing from the opposite side of the room, where Natalie was. I daresay I involuntarily took a step forward, and the man slipped past, behind me. It all happened so quickly, and I was so frightened, I can't describe my exact sensations. But I accept Madame Orienta's revelation as the truth, and—" Joyce's face paled a little, and she spoke very sternly, "I positively forbid any further investigation of the whole matter."

"Then you suspect some one?" asked Bobsy, quickly.

"Not at all," was the haughty answer, and Joyce looked like a queen issuing commands. "I have no idea who the intruder was, nor do I want to know. But if this story is made public, a dozen men will be found to fit the description, and it will mean no end of trouble and injustice. Therefore, I request, Mr. Roberts, that you let it go no further."

"I can't promise that," said Bobsy, gravely. "I am bound to report to my chief. But if he agrees, I will stop all investigation."

"That won't do," said Joyce, her dark eyes troubled. "You must promise what I ask."

"I think you need have no fear, Mrs. Stannard, of any injustice being done. One moment, Madame Orienta. You saw the footman, Blake, followed by Mrs. Faulkner, enter the room and turn on the' light, just as they testified?"

"The light was flashed on, and then I saw the servant, his hand still on the switch. Behind him, at his very shoulder, was Mrs. Faulkner, her face drawn with fear and horror. Naturally I turned my attention at once to the other end of the room, and there saw, for the first time, the two women whom I had heard enter a moment before."

"Thank you, that is all," and rising, Bobsy Roberts made brief adieus and hurried away.

He went straight to headquarters and sought Captain Steele.

"Got Stannard's murderer," he announced excitedly.

"Again or yet?" asked his unmoved listener.

"Got it in the queerest way, too," Bobsy went on, as he fished for his notebooks in the pocket of the overcoat he had laid off. "Do you believe in mejums, Cap?"

"Not so's you'd notice it. Spill your yarn."

"Well, to begin at the beginning of this chapter of it, Mrs. Stannard engaged a clairvoyant lady to see visions."

"Spooks?"

"Not exactly that, but to—well, to reconstruct the murder scene,—mentally, you know,—and see who did the stabbing. And by Jove, she told us!"

"Come now, Bobsy, I'll stand for a good deal from you—"

"Now, hold on, she didn't know she told——"

"What! Didn't know what she told—"

"If you could listen without butting in every minute, I'd give you the whole story."

"I'll try," and Captain Steele folded his hands and listened without a word while Bobsy told him every detail of the Orienta revelation.

Often he referred to his notes, and again he told vividly from memory the exact words of the priestess.

"And you fell for that?" cried Steele, as the tale ended.

"Sure I did, and so would you if you'd been there. You can sort of sense the difference between the professional fake mediums and this—this lady. She was the real thing, all right. I felt just as you do, before I saw her, but I was soon convinced. Why, man, that reading the sealed messages was enough."

"Pooh, they have lots of ways of doing that."

"But she didn't use any of their 'ways.' I, myself, handed the bunch to her, and immediately she read them out, and in pitch dark, too. No, there was no chance for trickery. She read them in dark or light, equally well. And not a seal broken or an envelope torn. Now, then!"

"No chance for a confederate?"

"Not the least. We sat in a row, and she sat facing us, fully eight feet away. And what could a confederate do? I handed her the envelopes,—she gave them back to me,— intact. Not one of us moved. When it was dark, her voice proved she was in her chair, and when I flashed on the light suddenly, there she was, without a change of posture, holding the envelopes exactly as I had given them to her. I tell you she's the real thing. I've read up on the trickery business, and all the books say that while there is lots of fraud, there is also a certain amount of telepathy or clairvoyance or whatever you call it, that's true. And that's her sort."

"Well, who is the man? Did she tell you?"

"No, she didn't know. But I know."

"Who, then?"

"Eugene Courtenay."

"What?"

"Of course it is. I've had him in the back of my head for some time, but I couldn't get a peg to hang a clue on. Now, I see how he could have done it. He did do it, just as the lady said. He slipped in, stabbed his man, turned off the light, and —slipped out again, past Mrs. Stannard."

"Why didn't she know it?"

"She did know it! Don't you see? Those two are in love. They wanted Stannard out of the way. But I don't think there was collusion. I think it was this way. You know, it is history that Mrs. Stannard and Courtenay were alone in the Billiard Room. Of course he was making love to her, and bemoaning the fact of Stannard's existence. Now, either he went from her into the studio, and she knew it, or else, he went away, as they say, and returned, through the Billiard Room—and she didn't know it."

"How could she help seeing him?"

"Oh, say she was crying,—or had buried her face in a sofa cushion,—or was sitting before the fire and he passed behind her. But admit that he could have gone through that room unknown to her,—which, of course, he could. Well, he goes in, and, later, in the dark, he goes out the same way. I don't know about her knowledge of any part of this performance, but I think she knew nothing of it, or she wouldn't have engaged the occult lady."

"She did that to clear herself."

"Yes, and Miss Vernon, too. But when the Priestess, as they call her, spoke of a tall, dark man, with a beard,

Mrs. Stannard was scared to death and wanted it all called off."

"A tall man, with a beard?"

"Yes, a dark, pointed beard! Isn't that Courtenay?"

"Sounds like him. Did she describe him further?"

"Yes, but only when I dragged it out of her. She vowed she couldn't see him clearly, and I pretended I wanted her to say a round, smooth-shaven face, and little by little I wormed it out, and it was Courtenay to the life. Then, Mrs. Stannard weakened on the whole show, which proves it."

"You say you've thought of him before?"

"Only vaguely. But you know his story. How he sat on the lawn bench and watched the lights go off and on! Good work, that! He himself turned them off and then escaped to the lawn, and cleverly sat there to see what occurred, instead of going home, and thereby being suspected,"

"And kept still when he found those two women were accused?"

"Sure. He knew they'd get off all right, and if he expected to marry Mrs. Stannard, he couldn't let himself get into the game. So he made up his simple, clever yarn, and stuck to it. Yes, sir, Courtenay's your man!"

"Wait, what about that conversation Mrs. Stannard overheard? She says her husband was talking to a woman."

"She made that up. Probably she had a glimmer of suspicion toward Courtenay, and did anything she could to make it seem somebody else."

"Then she hired this visionary, and that brought about the very revelation she didn't want!"

"But she never dreamed it would do so. She had no faith in the thing, and thought it would merely divert suspicion to some unknown intruder. And so it would, if I hadn't pinned the Seeress down to a careful description. Then, the more Mrs. Stannard showed discomfiture the more I knew I was right."

"I believe you, Bobsy. Now, how shall we go about proving it?"

"It will prove itself. It's a case of murder will out. You'll see!"

CHAPTER 13: AN ALIBI NEEDED

VERY discreetly Bobsy conducted his interview with Eugene Courtenay. The detective wanted to trap his man before he could realise any danger, so he called on him the morning after his talk with Steele.

Courtenay was not a business man. He called himself a farmer, but his farming was of the fancy variety and was done almost entirely by expert gardeners. His place was not far from the Folly, and when Bobsy called, at about eleven o'clock, he was received courteously enough by the man he desired to see.

"It's this way, Mr. Courtenay," said Bobsy, after a few preliminaries, "in the interests of law and justice, I want you to tell me a little more in detail the story you told at the inquest."

"There are no further details than those I related, Mr. Roberts. What have you learned that makes you think my testimony of sudden importance?"

Clearly, this was not a man to be easily hoodwinked. Bobsy felt his way. "Not of sudden importance. But all testimony is important, and sometimes by elaboration it becomes illuminative."

"Good word, illuminative," remarked Courtenay. "But I cannot help to shed light for you, I fear. Just what do you want to know?"

Here was an opening. Bobsy accepted it as such.

"At what time did you leave the Stannard house that night?"

"I don't know, really. One doesn't note hours when not on business matters. It must have been between eleven and half-past. That's as near as I can come to it. Why?"

The last word was shot at him, and Bobsy almost jumped.

"It is my duty to ask," he said coolly. "At what time did you reach home? I suppose you don't know that, either."

"I do not. But I didn't come home at once—"

"Yes, I know; you sat on a bench on the Folly lawn. Were you in evening togs, Mr. Courtenay?"

"I was."

"Had you on a hat?"

Eugene Courtenay started. But he answered at once: "Not a hat. I wore a cap over there. I often do when I go to a neighbour's."

"And you had it on when you sat on the bench?"

"Why, confound it, man. I don't know! I suppose I did. No, let me see. I believe I was carrying it, and laid it on the bench beside me."

"And left it there?"

Courtenay laughed a little self-consciously. "Yes, I did. I came nearly home before I thought of it. Then I went back and gathered it in. Why?"

Again that direct, snapped-out question.

"What was going on at the house when you went back?"

"How should I know? After events prove that the tragedy in the studio was then being gone through with— but I had no idea of that at the time. I glanced at the house, of course. There was a light in the studio—in fact, lights over most of the house. I found my cap and came on home. Why?"

"I'll answer your whys, Mr. Courtenay. Because the police have reason to think your story is not entirely true. Because we think it was you, yourself, who turned off the studio light."

"Do I understand, Mr. Roberts, you mean that I—let us speak plainly—that I killed Eric Stannard?"

"Did you, Mr. Courtenay?"

"I refuse to answer such an absurd question! In the first place, I was out on the lawn, when the light went out."

"So you say. But who corroborates that?"

"I was also out there when the light flashed on again."

"Yes, that may be true, but your first statement is not. You left Mrs. Stannard in the Billiard Room, you went into the studio—whether in the interim you had been out on the lawn or not, doesn't matter—you stabbed Eric Stannard, you turned off the light, and returning through the Billiard Room, you went back to that bench, and awaited developments."

"You must be insane!"

"Oh, no, I'm not jnsane. Neither were you. It was a clever dodge. You didn't know the women would be implicated, but when they were, however you might regret that, you couldn't confess your own guilt—"

"Why couldn't I?"

"Because," Bobsy looked squarely at him, "because you love Mrs. Stannard—"

"Stop! Don't you dare to speak her name! You mischief-maker! You absolute and unqualified—"

"Stop, yourself, Mr. Courtenay! These heroics harm your case—they don't help it."

"But it's false! It isn't true! I didn't do it! I was—"

"Yes?"

"I was on that bench all the time, till I went home—"

"Did you see any one, any servant or gardener, perhaps, who can vouch for your story?"

"No—I can't remember that I did. But, man, alive, how could I get in and out of that room? It has been proved—"

"It has been proved that you could have entered unseen and could have left unseen."

"But how?"

"Answer this question truthfully. What was Mrs. Stannard doing, when you left her in the Billiard Room?"

"She was sitting on one of the leather seats that are built to the wall."

"Was she looking at you, as you left?"

"No. She had buried her face in a pillow against which she leaned."

"Why did she do this? Was she feeling ill?"

"No."

"Then why the act?"

"I cannot say."

"You mean you will not. Was it because you had said something to her that caused her emotion?"

"I refuse to answer, and you have no right to ask."

"Very well, don't answer. But, you must admit, that if her face was buried in the pillow, she could not see if a man passed through the Billiard Room to the studio."

"But no one did!"

"How do you know?"

"Because I should have seen him from the bench where I sat."

"No, you would not, because you were the man."

"You accuse me?"

"I do."

"I deny it. But I shall say no more to you. Have you a warrant for my arrest?"

"I have not."

"Then go—and go quickly, before I tell you what I think of you!"

But Bobsy Roberts was no fool. He said, quietly, "I'd rather you would tell me what you think of me. It may help me to get at the truth. There are reasons why we are inquiring into your connection with this matter—you will hear the reasons soon enough. There is peculiar but direct evidence that you are the man who stabbed Mr. Stannard."

"Evidence? What do you mean?"

"Just what I say. But never mind that. You have nothing else to tell me? No proof to adduce that you were just where you claim to have been when the studio was darkened?"

"No! No proof, because none is needed. You can't have evidence—it is impossible!"

"Then that is all, Mr. Courtenay. You needn't tell me what you think of me. Your opinion doesn't interest me. But perhaps after you hear the evidence I speak of, you'll sing another tune. Oh, I'm not going to tell you about it. Ask Mrs. Stannard."

"I asked you not to mention that lady's name. Good-morning, Mr. Roberts."

"Good morning." And Bobsy went away, filled with conviction of Eugene Courtenay's guilt.

Courtenay went at once over to see Joyce.

"I've missed you so," she said, simply, as she met him on the Terrace. "Why haven't you been here?"

"I thought better not, darling. I can't control myself sufficiently to hide my love for you. And I feared it might bring embarrassment on you if I let it be seen by any one. Oh, Joyce, it seems so long to wait! Must it be two years? I can't live through it."

"Hush, Eugene. It seems sacrilege even to speak of our love and poor Eric dead so short a time. Be patient, dear heart. We are both young. You couldn't love me, or respect me, if I failed in ordinary behaviour toward a husband's memory. And Eric was good to me."

"Good to you! Losing his head over every pretty woman he met! Joyce, how could you ever marry him?"

"He made me. Don't you know how some women succumb to cave-man wooing? I don't understand it myself, but his whirlwind love-making carried me off my feet, and I had promised him before I knew it."

"If I had been here at the time, it would never have happened."

"I think it would. I was fascinated by his very vehemence. Now, I know better. I want only your gentle, dear love, that will comfort and content me as he never could."

"You poor little darling. I wish I could give it to you now. Mayn't I kiss you once—just once, Joyce?"

"No, Eugene. Not yet. Some day—when I can't be patient any longer. When the hunger for your big, sweet affection becomes too intense—the craving too uncontrollable."

She turned away from him and looked off toward the glowing richness of the autumn foliage.

"When the robins nest again," she said, with a little pathetic smile at the quotation. "But now, dear, sit down, I've a lot to tell you. I'm glad you came over, I was going to send for you."

And then, without further preamble, Joyce told him the whole story of Orienta and her revelations.

Courtenay listened, his eyes growing dark with anxiety as the story progressed.

"Who was the man?" he asked quietly, as she finished.

"Why, I don't know. Not a tramp, of course. But, perhaps some blackmailer. You know—Eric's life wasn't spotless."

"Listen, Joyce. The man, you say, was dark and with a pointed beard. He was in evening clothes, and wore no hat. He had reason to hate Eric Stannard. Do you know of any one who fulfils those conditions?"

Joyce looked at him, and a cloud of fear came to her beautiful eyes.

"Don't, Eugene," she cried, putting up her white hand, as if to ward off a blow. "Don't!"

"I must, Joyce. And you must listen. When I left you, did you keep your head down on that pillow—or, did you raise it? Tell me truly, dearest."

"I—I kept it down there. I was crying a little—after what—you know—what we had been talking about. I stayed that way a long time."

"Until you heard the sounds from the studio?"

"Yes; until that."

"Then some one could have passed you—you wouldn't have heard a soft step?"

"No, I probably shouldn't—but, Eugene, it wasn't you? Say it wasn't you!"

"It was not. But I have to prove this, Joyce— and it will be difficult."

"Oh, does any one think it was you?"

"Yes, the police think so."

"The police! That Roberts man! Oh, why— why did I ever have Madame Orienta come here? But we will prove it was not you, my Eugene—we will prove it."

"Yes, Joyce, my darling, we will, for we must. To whom have you told this story of sitting with your face bowed in the pillow?"

"To no one. Oh, yes, to the people in the house, of course. Barry and Beatrice, and, of course, little Natalie. Oh, Eugene, I was so glad when the Priestess' story seemed to clear Natalie and me of all suspicion of guilt. But if it has implicated you, that is a thousand times worse!"

"No, not worse. A man can fight injustice better than a woman. Have you told Roberts?"

"About the pillow? No, I don't think so. But he'll find it out. That man digs into everything."

"You invited him, yourself, to the seance?"

"Yes. I thought it wise. I thought it would implicate some stranger and I wanted him to hear."

"Why did you think it would accuse a stranger? Look here, Joyce, you didn't employ that woman to cook up a yarn, did you?"

"Mercy, no!" and Joyce opened her eyes full at him. "Eugene! What an idea! Of course I didn't. Why, I believe in her as fully as—as I do in you! I can't say more than that! She is honest and earnest in what she tells. Whether she sees truly, is another thing, and one over which she has no control. But all she says is in sincerity and truth."

"It may be. But she has surely woven a web around me. That is, if others share your belief in her. Now, I'm going to work, Joyce, to find my alibi."

"What do you mean?"

"I'm going to scare up somebody who saw me on that bench and will swear to it."

"Swear falsely?" Joyce whispered the words.

"If need be. But I hope to get an honest witness. May I speak to your outdoor servants? And the house staff, too, if necessary?"

"Of course. Find the head gardener, Mason, he'll round up the rest. Oh, Eugene, you will find some one, surely. They are about the grounds every night. And perhaps Barry saw you. He was out with the dogs."

"I'll find some one, dear. Don't worry."

Courtenay went away, and Joyce went into the house. She went to Beatrice Faulkner's room, and found her there.

"May I come in?" asked Joyce, at the door.

"Always, any time. Why, what is the matter, dear?"

"Beatrice! You don't think Eugene killed Eric, do you?"

"Of course not! What nonsense!"

"Well, they suspect him of it, and he's going to make up an alibi—or whatever you call it."

"Not make one up! Don't ever say that, Joyce. You mean, he's going to find proof of his own testimony."

"Yes, it's all the same. But, oh, Beatrice, if he did do it—I can never marry him—"

"Hush, Joyce! You mustn't talk like that! Don't you want to save Eugene?"

"Of course I do, if he's innocent."

"Then believe him innocent! You wrong-minded woman, to doubt the man who loves you, at the first breath of suspicion!"

"Then is he innocent, Beatrice? Is he?"

"Look in your heart and answer that yourself."

"I do look," said Joyce, solemnly, "but I can't read the answer."

Chapter 14: From Seven to Seventy

LISTEN, Joyce, dear. You are nervous and excited, or you never would do Mr. Courtenay such injustice. Think back; remember how he has always loved you—long before you married Eric. How patient and good he has been, never showing any undue interest in you or any animosity toward Eric. Why, then, imagine that he would do this desperate thing?"

"That's just it, Beatrice. He restrained his feelings as long as he could, and that night—in the Billiard Room, he—he lost control—and he said he—he c-couldn't stand it. You know he thought Eric didn't treat me right—"

"And Eric didn't. But even if Mr. Courtenay did lose his head for a moment, that doesn't mean he was the murderer, and you mustn't suspect him, Joyce."

"But you know what Orienta said—about a dark man with a pointed beard. Who else could it have been?"

"Other men have dark hair and beards. And Orienta couldn't see him clearly, you know."

"I know. And you are a comfort, Beatrice. But I never can marry Eugene if he has even a shadow of doubt hanging over him. I want him cleared."

"Of course you do. And as he is innocent, he will clear himself."

"Maybe not. If he can't find anybody who saw him out there on the bench, he will be arrested, and—"

"Oh, no, he won't. Why, somebody must have seen him!"

"If any of the servants had, they would have said so."

"They weren't asked. What about Barry?"

"Oh, I think Barry was off in the other direction, down by the orchards. But, Beatrice, maybe Mr. Wadsworth saw him. Didn't he leave you just about that time?"

"Yes, or a few moments sooner. Shall I ask him?"

"Oh, no. He's a fine man, and if he did see Eugene, his word will stand. Are you going to— do you care for him, Beatrice?"

"No, Joyce. He is, as you say, a fine man, and he has asked me many times to marry him, but I do not love him in that way. I admire and respect him, that is all."

"Poor Mr. Wadsworth. He worships the ground you walk on. Perhaps later, when all this horror is a thing of the past, you may change your mind."

"Never, Joyce. But I'll ask Mr. Wadsworth about Eugene. You telephone him to come over here. If I do—"

"He'll take it as encouragement. Yes, I know. I'll do it."

Joyce called him up on the telephone, and Wadsworth came over to the Folly that evening.

"Why, yes, I think so," he said, when questioned by Beatrice. "Let me see; when I left here, I walked a couple of times round the Italian garden paths, hesitating as to whether I should come back for one last appeal, or accept your refusal as final. I decided on the latter course, and was planning to go away on a long trip, to—to make myself keep away from you." He looked tenderly into the troubled face gazing into his own. "I don't want to persist too hard, dear, but I am of a determined nature, and I can't give you up. So, I'm going away, but I warn you I shall yet return and ask you once more—yes, once more, Beatrice."

"That is in the future," she returned, gravely, "but now, let us see if we can help poor Joyce."

"Poor Courtenay, as well! Now, I think I did see him, as I came along the South lawn. I'm sure I saw some man on the bench out there, and it was much the outline of Courtenay. And then, yes, I remember now, just then the light went out, and I couldn't see him clearly. Of course, I thought nothing of the light being put out. I assumed the people were going to bed, but it was that that decided me not to return to see you again that night. Had the lights stayed on, I fancy, after all, I should have entered the house again."

They were alone in the studio. It was but partially lighted, and Beatrice shuddered as she looked around the great apartment.

"Come out of here," she said; "I hate the place, it seems to be haunted by Eric's spirit. Come into the Reception Room."

Wadsworth followed as she went through the hall, but detained her a moment.

"What has become of your portrait painted on the staircase?" he asked.

"It's in the studio," she replied. "It isn't quite finished, you know."

"Mayn't I see it?"

"Not now. Some time."

"Stand on the stairs, the way the picture is painted."

Humouring his whim, Beatrice went up three steps and posed her hand on the balustrade, as Eric had painted her.

"Beautiful. Stannard was a wonderful genius. I want that picture, dear. I don't care if it is unfinished. If I can't have the original—yet—will you give me the duplicate?"

"No, oh, no I—" and Beatrice looked startled. "I'd hate you to have it, with this staircase and all—"

"I thought you loved this staircase—"

"As an architectural gem, yes. Mr. Faulkner prided himself on its design. But now—Eric's death—"

"Oh, yes, you stood right there, when your attention was first drawn to the footman's queer actions, didn't you?"

"Yes; I was just on this very step when I heard that faint moan—oh, don't remind me of it."

"I won't. I was a brute to be so thoughtless. Dear heart, can't you leave this house? Why do you stay in a place of such sad memories?"

"I do want to go away—and I must. And yet, Joyce needs me. She leans on me for everything. Come into this little room, and sit down."

They went into the cosy, low-ceiled Reception Room, and Beatrice continued. "I was just thinking I could leave her, when she became worried about Mr. Courtenay. Now, if you can convince the police that you saw him out there, just at that critical moment when the light disappeared, you will establish his alibi. Can you do this?"

"I'm sure I can. The more I think about it, the more I feel sure that it was Courtenay I saw."

"Had he a hat on?"

"No, but his hand on the back of the bench held a cap. I saw this clearly, for the light from the studio window was very strong. But as I looked at the man, the light went out. Understand, I was not looking at him with any curiosity or even interest. Merely he was in my line of vision, that is all. When I could not see him because of the sudden darkness, I thought no more of him, and I went home then."

"And you will go to the police and tell them this?"

"I certainly will, the first thing to-morrow morning. To-night, if you prefer."

"No, wait till morning. Stay here a little longer. I feel lonely to-night."

"Dear heart, can't you learn to look to me to cheer that loneliness?"

"Don't—you promised you wouldn't. But let's chat a bit. Tell me, do you believe at all in spiritism?"

"Spiritualism?"

"No; spiritism. They're quite different. Spiritualism is the old-fashioned table-tipping, rapping performance. Spiritism is the scientific consideration of life after death."

"Of course, I believe in life after death—"

"But do you think the dead can return and communicate with us?"

"By rapping and tipping tables?"

"No, not at all. By silent communion, or by a restless haunting of places they used to occupy? There! didn't you hear a faint sound then? A soft rustle, as of wings?"

"No, I didn't, and neither did you. That Orienta person has you all unnerved. I won't stand it. I insist on your leaving this house. If I see to it, that the police are fully informed of my evidence regarding Courtenay, will you get away at once?"

"I'd be glad to, if Joyce is willing I should go. Natalie is fond of me, too. But Barry will look after her. Yes, if Mr. Courtenay is freed of all suspicion, I will go away at once."

Roger Wadsworth's story carried weight with the police, who were already rather sceptical of testimony obtained from a clairvoyant.

And as Courtenay himself said to Captain Steele, "Your precious detective, Roberts, forced that woman to describe me. Even granting she had an hallucination, or whatever those people have, she didn't say anything about a pointed beard, or evening clothes and no hat, until he suggested it. Then she said 'yes.' If he'd said, 'hasn't he red hair and freckles?' she would have said 'yes,' also! It's auto-suggestion. Her mind was a blank, and any hint took form of a picture which she thought she saw. But since you've put me on the rack, I'm going into this thing myself. For reasons of my own, I'm going to hunt down the murderer of Eric Stannard. There's nobody on the job that has any push or perseverance. Young Stannard doesn't want the truth known. Why, I can't say. Nobody suspects him. But from now on, count on my untiring efforts. I'm ready to work with you, Captain Steele, or with Roberts, or any one you say. Or I'll work alone. But solve the mystery I'm bound to!"

Courtenay's manner went far to convince all who heard him of his own innocence, though Bobsy Roberts afterward growled something about "protesting too much." But when Courtenay said he would be at their bidding if they learned anything against him, they agreed to let him go in peace to pursue his own inquiries.

And he went first to Lawyer Stiles, to look into the matter of Stannard's will.

"The first motive to consider," Courtenay said to the surprised lawyer, "is always a money motive. Who benefits by this will, aside from the principals?"

Stiles produced the document, and they went over its possibilities. Suddenly Courtenay started in astonishment.

"Have you noticed anything peculiar about this will?" he asked.

The lawyer looked at him with a somewhat blank expression.

"Just what do you mean?" he said.

"Ah, then you have seen it! Were you going to let it pass unnoted?"

"I must ask you to explain your enigmatical remarks."

"And I will do so. That will has been tampered with, and you know it!"

"Tampered with?"

"Don't repeat my words like a parrot! Yes, tampered with. The original, written in Mr. Stannard's own hand, has been added to by some one else."

"What makes you think so?"

"I don't think so, I know so. Now, why haven't you made it known? You must have seen it?"

"Where is the fancied alteration?"

Courtenay looked at the stern face of the lawyer, and wondered if he could be dishonest or if he had been blind. He laid his finger on one clause, the one stating Natalie Vernon's bequest, and said, "There, that is the place. That was written seven thousand dollars, it has been changed to read seventy thousand dollars."

Lawyer Stiles peered at the words through his rubber-rimmed glasses. "It is in letters and figures both," he demurred, "it would be difficult—"

"I know it is. And it was not very difficult to add ty to the written seven, and there chanced to be room for an extra cipher after the original naughts, thus giving the inheritor ten times as much as was intended by the testator."

"Well?"

"Well, do you, as a reputable lawyer, admit that you overlook a palpable fraud like that?"

"I'm sorry you saw that, Mr. Courtenay. In explanation, I have nothing to say, but justice to myself compels me to remind you that I am in the confidence of the Stannard family, and this is their affair—not yours."

"Whew!" Courtenay gave a short whistle. "I begin to see. They know it, and make no objection."

"Y—yes."

"Who knows it?"

"Barry Stannard."

"And Mrs. Stannard?"

"I can't say. She read the will, but made no comment."

"You're sure Barry knows?"

"I am."

"And he stands for it because Miss Vernon did it! That baby! Who'd think her capable of such a thing?"

"Hush, Mr. Courtenay. You've no right to accuse her. You've no evidence that she did it. In fact, I'm told Miss Vernon writes a large, dashing hand, and this—"

"And Eric Stannard's hand is small and cramped. Yes, a clever forgery. It looks quite a bit like his own writing. But the ink is different, the slant is different, why, a half blind man could see the words have been changed!"

"Granting that. What matter, if Barry Stannard doesn't care? Moreover, he is going to marry Miss Vernon, and the fortune will be theirs jointly."

"But don't you see? If Natalie Vernon altered that will, she wanted that larger sum, and— she—"

"Don't say it. At least, don't say it to me. If you want to put the matter up to Barry, go ahead. But I decline to express an opinion or form a conclusion."

"What does Barry say?"

"He ignores it. I called his attention to it, and he said, 'Changed figures? Oh, I guess not. It doesn't matter, anyway; that, and more, will be at Miss Vernon's disposal some day.' So I said no more."

Eugene Courtenay went straight to Joyce.

"Do you know anything about a changed figure in Eric's will?" he asked, bluntly.

"No," she returned; "what do you mean?"

"Natalie Vernon altered her bequest from seven thousand dollars to seventy thousand."

"How could she?"

"It wasn't difficult. Eric wrote the will himself. He wrote seven and she made it seventy—the words, I mean. Then he wrote a figure seven and three ciphers, and she squeezed in another cipher. Mighty clever work, but as plain to be seen as a blot on a letter."

"What possessed the child?"

"Don't call her a child. The woman who could and would do that, is a Machiavelli in petticoats. But don't you see where the knowledge of her act leads us?"

"You mean—" Joyce could not say it.

"Of course I do. I've thought all along there was still a doubt of her."

"Oh, I haven't. Even if she did alter the will, that doesn't prove—"

"It doesn't prove—anything. But you know this will was made very recently—"

"Of course; Natalie has only been here two months."

"I know it. Well, say, Eric made this bequest of her, soon after she came—you know, Joyce, he was crazy over her from the very beginning—"

"Yes, I know it, Eugene."

"And then, when she got a chance, she changed it, and, why, why would she do this, except to inherit—at once?"

"Natalie! That dear little thing! Never! I did suspect her the least mite, just at first—but I don't now."

"Barry does."

"Oh, no! He can't."

"He does. And that's why he didn't want any fuss made about her forgery——"

"Don't call it that!"

"It is that. What else can I call it?"

"But I can't believe it. Maybe—maybe somebody else did it. Barry—"

"Nonsense! Why should Barry do it, when he fully intended to marry her?"

"Oh, I don't know! It's all so confusing."

"Not confusing; there's no doubt she did the forging. But it's a terrible state of affairs. I don't want to be the one to accuse her."

"Must you?"

"Well, I'd determined to sift things to the bottom to lay my hand on Eric's murderer. Primarily to clear myself—for your sake. And, too, for the sake of justice and right. I'll go now, Joyce, I must think this out alone. Good-bye, darling. Don't worry. I'll do only what is right, and—what you approve."

Chapter 15: Natalie in Danger

NATALIE! What are you doing?" Joyce entered Natalie's room, to find her on her knees before an open trunk. Hats and gowns lay about the room, the wardrobe shelves were empty, and as the girl was fairly flinging wearing apparel into the tills, the question was superfluous.

"I'm packing," the model answered, "to go away."

"Why, what has happened? Why do you want to go?"

Natalie rose to her feet. A negligee of pale green Liberty silk fell in lovely folds about her, her slender arms were bare, and her gold hair hung in two long braids.

"I can't stand it any longer, Joyce," she said, her voice quivering. "It's all so dreadful. Suspicion everywhere, and everybody looking on me as a murderer, and—"

"Now, Natalie, dear, don't talk like that. And, anyway, you can't go. I don't believe they'd let you—"

"Why not? I'm not under arrest, or surveillance, or whatever they call it.'

"You would be, if you tried to go away. Don't you know we are all watched—whatever we do or wherever we go?"

"But they don't suspect you any more, Joyce, and you were found just as near Eric as I was, when— when he—"

"Hush, Natalie, you don't know what you're talking about. Why, now they suspect Eugene."

"I know they do, but he didn't do it. He'll soon convince them of that."

"I'm not sure that he can. And—suppose he did do it"

"Kill Eric? Joyce, you're crazy! Why would he?"

"You know, well enough—"

"That he loved you, yes, but that wouldn't make him commit crime. Why, you wouldn't marry him if he won you in that way."

"Of course, I wouldn't. And that's what's worrying me. If he and Eric quarrelled about me, and if—oh, I can't tell you just what I mean—"

"I know. If Eugene reproved Eric for his neglect of you, or—for his attentions to me, it might have led to high words, and Mr. Courtenay is a very impetuous man, and Eric never would brook a word of criticism—oh, of course I understand, Joyce!"

"But Eugene must be cleared—he must be, at any cost. Look here, Natalie, did you know Eric had left you such a big bequest?"

Natalie flushed, and began to walk nervously up and down the room. "Why," she said, not looking at Joyce, "he told me he'd leave me a nice little sum, but he said he wasn't going to die till he was ninety, so I didn't pay much attention to the matter."

"But didn't you know the sum he mentioned in his will? Had he never told you?"

"Why do you ask that?"

"Because that will was altered. The sum he wrote for you was made ten times greater."

"Was it?" Natalie spoke slowly, as if to gain time.

"Yes, it was. You knew this?"

"How could I know it? I never saw the will."

"They think you did. They think you altered it."

"Who thinks so?"

"The police and Mr. Stiles. And Eugene asked me about it. I thought I'd ask you before anybody else did."

"That was dear of you, Joyce." Natalie sat down on a couch, and taking her chin in her two palms, sat silent a moment. "Joyce," she said, at last, "why are you good to me? You think I killed Eric—"

"No, I don't, Natalie—— But, oh, don't you see? I don't want to think it was Eugene, and— I don't know which way to turn."

"You're not in such a terrible strait as I am, Joyce," and Natalie's blue eyes turned dark with sadness unutterable. "I don't know what to do— I've no one to ask, no one to confide in—"

"Can't you tell me?"

"You, least of all. Mrs. Faulkner is a dear, but she is so unwilling to admit she suspects anybody— I mean, anybody we know. She insists it was some stranger—and, it wasn't—I mean—oh—what am I saying? Joyce, I shall go crazy."

Natalie looked distraught. Her eyes had a wild look, as of a hunted animal. Her little fingers plucked at the silk of her robe, and her slippered foot tapped the rug continuously.

"You didn't love Eric, did you?" and Joyce looked at the girl, as if seized with a new idea.

"No! I hated him! Forgive me, Joyce, but I can't help it. He was almost repulsive to me. Not physically—he was handsome, and most correctmannered, and all that. But I was afraid of him. I've only posed for a few artists, but they were all—you know—impersonal in their relations with me. But Eric made love to me from the first."

"I know it. I saw it."

"And you didn't resent it?"

"I felt more pity for you than jealousy of you. I know Eric, and oh, Natalie, I tried so hard to be good, and to do my duty—but Eugene was always around, you know— and, must I confess it? I was rather glad that Eric's attention was taken up with his model."

"I know. I saw all that. But you see, I care for Barry. And Eric told me—"

"What, Natalie?"

"No, I can't tell you. Oh, Joyce, I am in danger. I can't ward it off, and I can't meet it. What shall I do? What can I do?"

"May I come in?" and Barry appeared at the door of the boudoir.

"Yes," Joyce answered. "Come on in. This child says she is going away."

"She isn't!" and Barry slammed the trunk lid shut, turned the key, removed it and put it in his pocket.

"Oh," cried Natalie, forced to smile at this highhanded piece of business. "There's a lot of things in there I want!"

"Can't have 'em," returned Barry, "unless you promise to put 'em back in that very empty wardrobe I see yawning at us."

"Barry, I must go away. I've—I've good reasons."

Joyce had left the room, and Barry sat down beside the trembling little figure and put an arm round her.

"Don't speak of going away, Natalie. Don't think of it. It would look like confession."

"Have you heard about the will?" she asked, an awestruck note in her voice.

"Yes, but never mind about that. When we can get married, all my half the fortune will be yours anyway. That item of seven thousand or seventy thousand makes no difference to us."

"But you don't think I—forged it—do you, Barry?"

"Of course not, darling. I don't think you ever did a wrong thing in your life, of any sort or description—and I wouldn't care if you had."

"Wouldn't you care if I had committed—crime?"

"Oh, if you put it that way, I suppose I'd care— but I'd love you just the same."

"Just the same?"

"Just exactly, darling."

"And you don't think I changed that will?"

"I do not."

"Who did, do you think?"

"How do you know anybody did?"

"Joyce says so."

"Well, never mind about it. If I know who did it, I won't tell you—and you needn't ask."

"It was a very strange thing for anybody to do, Barry."

"Except you—"

"Yes, except me! Oh, you do think I did it!"

"Hush, sweetheart, don't talk so loud. Now, listen, Natalie. You're in a tight place. There's no use denying it, you are. Now I want you to promise me to do exactly as I tell you, in every instance. You trust me to do only what is best for both of us, don't you?"

"For both of us—yes, Barry." The blue eyes were very sad, but the soft voice did not falter.

"That's a trump, my own little trump! There are some dark hours ahead, darling. I don't know just how things will turn. But I'm tying to head off trouble, and I hope to succeed."

"Barry, Eugene Courtenay didn't kill Eric, did he?"

"No, Natalie, he didn't. That clairvoyant business was all poppycock."

"Then how did she read those questions, Barry? I think that was wonderful."

"It was, Natalie. I concede you that. She couldn't have used any trickery there—there was absolutely no chance."

"She really read them, then, by clairvoyant sight?"

"I don't see any other explanation."

"Nor do I. Then, why wasn't her vision of the—the scene in the studio, the truth?"

"I don't say it wasn't. I don't say but what somebody did slip past Joyce and get into the room that way. But it wasn't Courtenay."

"I don't think it was, either."

"Of course you don't. Now, my own little girl, remember, you've promised me—I—"

"To love, honour and obey you—"

"You darling!" and Natalie's speech was interrupted by an impulsive kiss. "You blessed angel! But you mustn't say such things, they unnerve me— and I've a hard row to hoe, my girl."

"Can't I help?"

"Only by doing the things you just promised to do. I want you to, of course; it was only the suggestion in the phrase you used that drove me crazy! Some day, sweetheart, you shall promise before witnesses; but just now, swear to me alone, that you will obey my least dictate in this—this trouble."

"I will, Barry," and, solemnly, Natalie lifted her scarlet, curved lips for the kiss that sealed the compact.

"Mr. Roberts is here," said Joyce, looking in at the door; "he wants to see Natalie."

"Oh, I can't see him!" and Natalie clung tremblingly to Barry, "what shall I do?"

"Do just as I tell you, dearest. See him, of course. And—"

"Then I'll have to dress. Go on down, Barry, and talk to him till I come."

Natalie seemed to turn brave all in a moment at Barry's words. Stannard went downstairs, and Joyce helped the girl to slip into a house-gown.

"A pretty one," she stipulated. "I want him to like me."

"As if any one could help doing that," and Joyce selected a little grey velvet, with lots of soft lace falling away from the round-cut bodice.

"There," she said, as Natalie hastily twisted up her hair and thrust a couple of shell pins in it, "you look a dream! a demure little dream. Natalie, be careful, won't you?"

The girl gave Joyce a long look, and said softly, "Yes—for his sake." Then she went slowly downstairs.

Bobsy Roberts was talking with Mrs. Faulkner as Natalie entered. He jumped up, and greeted the lovely girl with an impulsive, "So sorry to trouble you, but I must ask you a question or two, and I promise to cut it short."

"What is it?" and Natalie gave him one of her confiding smiles.

Bobsy hesitated. How could he ask a fairy like that, a rude, blunt question. But it had to' be done, and he said, "It's—it's about Mr. Stannard's will. Did you ever see it?"

Clearly, Natalie was surprised. It seemed to be not the query she had looked for. But she was calm. After the slightest pause, she said slowly, very slowly, as if choosing her words, "No, Mr. Roberts, I have never seen Mr. Stannard's will. Why should I see it?"

"You know he left you a large sum of money?"

"Of course I know that. Mr. Stiles informed me.

"Did you not know of it before Mr. Stiles told you?"

Natalie glanced at Barry, who smiled at her.

"Yes; that is, I knew Mr. Stannard had left me a bequest, but I did not know how much. Nor did I care!" Natalie lost her self-control. "Do you suppose I wanted that money? I did not, and I do not! I refuse to take it!"

"My dear child," said Beatrice Faulkner, rising and going to sit beside her, "don't say such things. The money is honestly yours—"

"Not so fast, Mrs. Faulkner," said Roberts, amazed at Natalie's excited words; "we cannot feel sure the money honestly belongs to Miss Vernon until we know who altered Mr. Stannard's will. Did you?"

He turned quickly to Natalie with his question, as if anxious to get the miserable business over.

"Certainly not," she replied, with disdain in every line of her face. "In the first place, Mr. Bobsy—I mean, Mr. Roberts—"

The light laugh that greeted her slip of the tongue served to break the tension of the moment. "Forgive me," she said, and her dimpling smile of embarrassment would have turned the head of an anchorite. "You see, I've heard you called that, and, though I didn't mean to be familiar, I—I got sort of mixed up."

"All right, Miss Vernon, it doesn't matter at all. One Robert's as good as the other."

"It's funny to have two names alike, isn't it?" and Natalie's voice shook a little.

"Yes," and then with an effort, Bobsy returned to the attack. "You know nothing of the change in the will, then, Miss Vernon?"

"I certainly don't. Did somebody change the text?"

"Yes. It's a mysterious affair. But if you know nothing about it, we must ferret it out as best we can."

He spoke lightly, but his eyes never left Natalie's face. In fact, Roberts was by no means asking her because he attached any importance to her spoken answer, but because he hoped by her expression or by some inadvertent slip, to learn the truth, even though she tried to conceal it.

"Mr. Roberts," she said, suddenly, "if I wish to go away from this house, is there any reason I should not do so?"

"I'd rather you would ask somebody else that, Miss Vernon."

"Whom shall I ask?"

"Captain Steele, or—"

"I am answered. You mean I would not be allowed to go."

"I think it would be better for you to remain where you are. There may be developments shortly, that will call for your presence, though they may not affect you seriously. Please don't plan to go away just now, but, also, don't think my advice more indicative than it is meant to be."

Roberts went off, and the four people he left behind him sat in a constrained silence.

At last, Beatrice spoke. "We must all band together to save Natalie," she said, very seriously. "There is no use deceiving ourselves; Natalie is in danger. We know and love her, so we can't connect her in our minds with any wrong-doing, but to outsiders the case looks different. Let us, then, face conditions that exist, and plan how we can best help her."

"There's only one way," said Joyce, "and that is to find the real murderer. I wish I had never let that Orienta mix herself into the matter. It's her talk that turned suspicion toward Eugene. And we all know he's innocent. But when we try to find out who is the criminal, Eugene's name comes up."

"I'm not sorry we had the clairvoyant," said Beatrice, thoughtfully. "As you say, we all know Mr. Courtenay is innocent, but if there was an intruder, Orienta explained how he could have entered. You wouldn't have heard any one pass you in the Billiard Room that night, would you, Joyce?"

"No, I'm sure not; I was—I was crying—and I gave no thought to anything but my own troubles."

"Then somebody may have slipped by you—of course, not Mr. Courtenay, but somebody—"

"I wish that woman had seen the intruder's face," said Natalie, suddenly. "You know, I believe in clairvoyance—I'm psychic myself—I wonder—oh, I wonder if I could find out anything—in that way!"

"What are you talking about?" said Barry, impatiently. "Don't you mix yourself up in those witchcraft things—"

"'Tisn't witchcraft. And, anyway, I've a notion to try it. Don't you think I might, Mrs. Faulkner?"

"Might what, dear?"

"Find out something about the mysteries that are growing deeper and more numerous all the time?"

"I don't know, I'm sure," began Beatrice, with a helpless look, but Barry said, sternly, "I forbid it," and turning on his heel, he left the room.

CHAPTER 16: CONFESSION AND ARREST

THAT evening Barry Stannard was not at home, and Natalie declared her intention of trying to learn something by psychic or clairvoyant revelation. The three women sat in the Billiard Room, and were for the thousandth time discussing the tense situation.

"Why, if you want to try it, Natalie, go ahead," said Joyce, wearily. "It certainly can't do any harm. Barry only objects because he thinks it will get you into a nervous state—"

"Nonsense! It makes me more nervous to be forbidden to do what I wish. Come on, let's go in the studio, and try it, at any rate."

"I'd rather not," said Beatrice Faulkner. "In a way, Barry has asked me to keep you from this sort of thing, and I feel a certain responsibility—"

"I understand," said Natalie; "and you needn't take any part. Just sit by and look on."

"No, I'd rather not. If you don't mind, I'll go to my room. I've letters to write, and I'm sure you'll get along better without a disturbing element."

"I agree with Beatrice," Joyce said, after she had gone. "If you can do anything at all, you can do it better with only approving minds present. What are you going to do, anyway? I mean, how are you going to attempt it?"

"I'm not sure, but I think I can go into a trance, like Orienta did—"

"She didn't go into a trance."

"Not exactly. But she had a sort of trancelike condition come over her. Well, come on in the studio, and I'll see."

The two went into the big room, and Natalie sat down in a small chair, directly facing the chair in which Eric

Stannard had died. She held in her hand the scratched and defaced etched picture of herself.

"You sit beside me, Joyce. I somehow feel if you hold my hand it will help. Now I'll concentrate on the etching, and perhaps there will be a manifestation of some sort from Eric, or I may have a vision—of the truth."

Interested, but not very hopeful of success, Joyce sat beside the girl, and they concentrated their thoughts on the empty chair in front of them and the man who used to use it.

For ten minutes they sat in silence. Natalie quivered and occasional shudderings shook her slender frame, but there was no trance or vision. And then, just as Joyce was about to exclaim that she could bear it no longer, her nerves were giving way, they heard a sound that was exactly the same as the sighing groan that had reached their ears when Eric was dying. Startled, they gazed wildly at each other, then back to the great armchair. Was his spirit still hovering about the place it had last been in the flesh? Again they waited, and again they heard that ghastly sound. Faint, almost inaudible, but unmistakably the voice of the dying man. It seemed to say "Help!" but so low was the tone they could scarce be sure. And then the light went out and they were in utter darkness.

Natalie gasped out a faint scream, and Joyce gripped her hand, with a whispered, "Huh! Don't scream! The servants will come in. I'll make a light."

She rose and tremblingly made her way across the room to the main switch. It was turned off, and with a twist, she flashed on the light. Quickly she stepped out into the hall. There was no one there but Blake, and as the door had been closed, he had noticed nothing. He said nobody had passed through the hall.

Upstairs Joyce ran, conscious only of a desire to find some one who would admit having turned off the light. She ran to Beatrice Faulkner's room and entered without knocking.

"What is it?" said Mrs. Faulkner, looking up from the letter she was writing, "Oh, Joyce, what has happened?"

"Somebody turned off the studio lights! Beatrice, who could have done it?"

"Turned off the lights! What do you mean?"

"Yes, Natalie and I sat there, Natalie thought she would go into a trance, you know—"

"That foolish girl! Did she?"

"No. But we heard—oh, I can't tell you now! Come with me back there, do!"

Rising hastily from her desk, Beatrice followed Joyce downstairs and into the studio. There they found Natalie standing by a table in the middle of the room, looking with a staring gaze at a large leather case that was on the table.

"The jewels!" cried Joyce. "Eric's jewels! Where did you find them, Natalie?"

"Right here on this table. I haven't touched them."

"What do you mean?" and Beatrice looked curiously at the girl. "How did they get there?"

"I don't know," said Natalie, dully. She seemed as one bereft of her senses. "When Joyce turned on the lights—"

"Who turned them off?" put in Beatrice, unable to hold back the question.

"Eric did," said Natalie, her eyes wide with awed wonder. "He—that is, his spirit, was here—we heard him sigh—and he turned the lights off and then put the jewels on the table—"

"Oh, Natalie, what nonsense! It couldn't have been Eric's spirit that brought that box in here!"

"Then who did?"

Beatrice looked at the girl, and said, "Did you do it, Natalie? Did you know where they were all the time?"

"No, I didn't do it. Neither did Joyce. We sat right there by Eric's chair—and Eric was present—we heard him, didn't we, Joyce?"

"We did, Beatrice, we surely did. I'd know that voice among a thousand. It was the same groan— the same cry for help that he uttered that—that awful night. Can it be that he came back at Natalie's wish?"

"It's too incredible," returned Beatrice. "I can't believe it. Joyce, it must have been one of the servants, who turned off the light and put the box in here. One who had stolen it."

"No, Blake saw nobody."

"Was he in the hall?"

"Yes, just where he was that other night. Oh, it's too weird. I don't know what to think!"

"Maybe some one came in from outside—"

"No, we were as silent as death itself. We would have heard a window or door open. There was no sound whatever, was there, Natalie?"

"No. Spirits make no sound."

The girl was still in a half-dazed state. Almost in a trance she was, even now, or, rather, she appeared so.

"I can't stand it," she said. "I feel giddy. I'll go to my room."

She went away, and the two other women stood, looking at each other.

"It must have been Natalie," said Joyce, reluctantly. "You see, she did know where the jewels were and got them out of some hiding-place when I ran up to your room."

"But how could she turn off the lights?"

"I don't know, unless she has an accomplice among the servants. Sometimes I think Blake—"

"No, Joyce, don't implicate Blake. I feel sure he is entirely innocent. Did you hear that voice clearly?"

"Not clearly, but unmistakably. As I say, it was so still that every sound seemed exaggerated. But I heard Eric's voice as truly as I stand here. Explain it, Beatrice."

"How can I? Except to say that there must have been some human agency. I don't believe for a minute that Eric's ghost returned the jewels."

"But Natalie says he has haunted this studio ever since he died. She says he will continue to do so, until his murderer is found and punished."

"I have heard of such things, but I can't believe it in this case."

"What will Barry say? He was so imperative that Natalie should not try the trance business."

"I know it. But I can't see that she has done any real harm. The jewels are here—isn't it marvellous, Joyce? How could they have been brought in without your knowing it?"

"Oh, as to that, I'm sure Natalie produced them after I left the room. I wish now I'd stayed here. My one thought was to get somebody else to corroborate the mysterious happenings."

"You're sure the jewels were not here on the table when you went out of the room?"

"I can't say positively. They might have been. You see, I never thought of looking for them. I looked about the room to see if any person were present, and I looked thoroughly, too. But I didn't look on the table."

"Nobody could have come in at the Billiard Room door?"

"No, we sat right there, you know. The case is just the same as on the night of the murder. That's why Natalie insists that Eric's spirit turned off the lights and put the jewels on the table."

"Are the jewels all there? Are any missing?"

"I've not looked them over. At a first glance, they seem to be all right."

"It must be that some one stole them, and just now returned them. There's no other possible explanation, Joyce. It throws suspicion back to Mr. Truxton or—"

"Or Eugene Courtenay, you were going to say! Now, he didn't do it, Beatrice—I know he didn't."

Weary and afraid, full of nameless horrors and uncertainties, Joyce locked the jewels in her dressing-room safe, and went to bed.

She and Beatrice both felt they could stand no more that night, and notifying the police of the finding of the jewels must wait until the next day.

And next day, when Bobsy Roberts came and heard the strange story he was probably the most bewildered man on the force.

"Tell it all over again," he said, after hearing the tale from Joyce.

Patiently she repeated the details.

"Where is Miss Vernon?" he asked abruptly.

"You can't see her to-day," returned Joyce, "the poor child is prostrated."

"What did she hope to gain by her trance performance?" asked Roberts, mulling over Joyce's story.

"She hoped to get some sort of manifestation that would tell her who was the murderer. She never thought of having the jewels restored."

"Now, Mrs. Stannard, there's no use trying to dodge the issue. We've been pretty suspicious of Miss Vernon from the first. This last matter settles it, to my mind. You know that unsent letter found in Mr. Stannard's desk was without doubt meant for Miss Vernon. You know it said that she knew where the jewels were hidden. Now, she has proved that she did know, and she produced them in this hocus-pocus way, to hide her theft."

"No, no, Mr. Roberts, I cannot believe it! Natalie is not bad enough for all that maneuvering; nor would she, I'm sure, be capable of it. Again, granting you're right in suspecting her of making up last evening's events, how could she imitate Mr. Stannard's voice—"

"Oh, that was hypnotism. Miss Vernon is psychic, and, too, she evidently possesses the power of hypnotising at will. She made you believe you heard those sounds. She made you believe the lights went out—"

"Oh, I know the light went out! I couldn't be mistaken as to that!"

"No, but I mean she went and turned them out while you thought she still sat by your side. Weren't your eyes closed?"

"No, they were wide open. She did not leave her seat. The lights were turned off by a hand other than hers, whether mortal or spirit, I cannot say."

"Well, the whole affair was of her invention and carrying out. She is responsible for your husband's death, Mrs. Stannard. There is no doubt whatever of Miss Vernon's guilt."

"Just take that back, Roberts," and Barry Stannard came into the Reception Room where the speakers were sitting. "Miss Vernon is as innocent as an angel in this business. I'm ready to confess. I killed my father, and I own up to it, rather than have Natalie suspected. If you had been any sort of a detective you would have known from the first that I did it. But you had your head set in one direction and nothing could change you. You know perfectly well I had motive and opportunity. It was not premeditated, I did it on the spur of sudden indignation."

"Barry," cried Joyce, "what are you saying? You didn't kill Eric!"

"Yes, I did. I thought it might blow over and remain an unsolved mystery. But if Natalie is to be suspected of my crime, I would be less than a man to keep still. Take me along, Roberts, I give myself up."

Bobsy Roberts stared at him. "My plan worked," he said, slowly. "I thought it was you, really, all along, but I thought, too, the only way to get a confession from you, was to seem to suspect Miss Vernon. As you say, no man could sit still and see a woman bearing the blame that belongs to him. You came in through the Billiard Room?"

"Yes," said Barry. "Mrs. Stannard didn't see or hear me pass her. I went on through to the studio. I accused my father of persecuting Miss Vernon, and he turned on me in a furious rage. We are both impetuous, we said little, but those few low words roused all my worst nature, and, snatching up the etching needle, I stabbed him, scarce knowing what I did. It was all over in a moment, and I had but one thought, how to escape from that room. I flew across and turned off the lights as a precautionary measure, and then—"

"Then how did you get out?" asked Bobsy, breathless with interest.

"I was behind the hall door, when Blake opened it, and after he turned on the light, I slipped behind him and Mrs. Faulkner out into the hall. They were so bewildered at the sudden flash of light— and—what it revealed, that they didn't see me at—"

"Barry!" exclaimed Joyce, "I would have seen you if you had done that."

"No, you had eyes for nothing but Eric's wounded body. You couldn't have torn your gaze from that if you had wanted to."

"What did you do after leaving the room?" asked Roberts.

"I went out and walked about the lawn. My head was spinning round from excitement and shock at my own deed."

"You stayed near the house?"

"Yes, Halpin came out and found me. He told me what had happened and I went right back into the studio."

"You have kept this secret so long. Why?"

"Surely you can understand. I love Miss Vernon. I want to marry her. Can I ask her to marry a murderer?"

"You mean if she knows it?"

"I mean if she knows it. I wanted to keep the secret forever, I hoped to do so. When she was suspected last week, I felt sure she would be cleared. Then when the will was seen to be changed——"

"One moment. Did you change the will?"

"I did."

"What for?"

"Because of what has just now happened. If I had to confess, of course, I could never marry Miss Vernon. And in that case, I wanted her to be provided for."

"That will cannot stand."

"I don't care anything about that. I've confessed now, my life is practically ended. I can will my own fortune to Miss Vernon."

"And the jewels? Did you return those last night? And the emeralds to Mrs. Stannard last week?"

"No," said Barry, slowly. "I don't know anything about the jewels. Perhaps there was a robber, after all. Say a jewel fancier—"

"Or say a little girl who was fond of jewelry."

"No," and Barry shook his head, "Miss Vernon knew nothing of the jewels."

"But the letter to her—"

"That letter wasn't to her, it was to some woman my father knew and feared. He never would have given the emeralds to Natalie. The idea is preposterous."

"That must be found out. Then the rigamarole the clairvoyant told was true, about a man coming into the studio"

"Yes, it was all true. I was the man."

Barry's voice was infinitely sad and despairing. Joyce looked at him pityingly. His white face was drawn and his eyes were full of grief. "I think, Mr. Stannard, if all you've told me is true, I must ask you to go with me to Headquarters."

"I am ready," said Barry, simply, and the two men went out.

CHAPTER 17: ALAN FORD

JOYCE went up to Natalie's room and found the girl sitting up in bed trying to eat some of the dainty breakfast a maid had just brought her. A cap of lace and tiny rosebuds confined the gold hair, and a breakfast jacket of pale blue brocade was round her shoulders.

"Joyce," she said, staring at her with big blue eyes, "where did those jewels come from?"

"I don't know, Natalie. It's the most mysterious thing I ever heard of. But listen, dear, I've something to tell you. Barry has confessed—"

"What!" Natalie almost shrieked the word. "What do you mean?"

"Just what I say. Barry has confessed that he killed his father. You suspected him all the time, didn't you?"

"Did you?"

"Oh, I couldn't—and yet who else could it have been? I did think of Barry at first, and then I decided it couldn't be."

"And then you suspected me?"

"Oh, Natalie, how can I say? I did and I didn't. I had no notion which way to turn. But now, even though he says so, I can't believe it was Barry."

"Barry! Of course it wasn't Barry!"

"But he confessed, Natalie."

"Of course he confessed. He couldn't help it!" As she spoke, Natalie was getting out of bed, and seating herself at her dressing table began to do up her hair. "If you don't mind going, Joyce, I want to dress. Run along now, I'll be down very soon."

"What are you going to do?" Joyce looked at the girl uncertainly, for she was brushing her hair with unwonted vigour. Her eyes were tear-filled, but her face showed a brave, determined expression, and she hurried her toilet as if important matters impended.

"Go now, Joyce," and rising, Natalie pushed her gently toward the door.

Some minutes later, Natalie came downstairs, in a trim out-of-door costume. Her smart little hat was veiled, and she had a motor coat over her arm.

"May I take the little electric, Joyce, and drive it myself?"

"Why, yes, of course. Where are you going?"

"First, to see Mr. Roberts. And if I'm not home for some hours, don't be alarmed. I may go to—' well, I may take a long drive. But I'll be back to dinner."

In a moment Joyce saw the little electric coupe whirling down the drive.

Straight to Headquarters Natalie went, and found Bobsy Roberts.

"Barry Stannard didn't kill his father," she said, without preamble. "You had no right to arrest him."

"But he confessed the crime, Miss Vernon."

"Don't you know why he did that?" The lovely eyes fell before Bobsy's surprised glance.

"No, why? If he is not the criminal?"

"Of course he isn't. He said all that to—to save me."

Bobsy looked sharply at her. "Is that so? And how am I to know that you're not telling me this to save him?"

"You can't know! That's just it. You've not wit enough to know what is the truth and what isn't."

"Thank you for the implied compliment."

"Don't be sarcastic. This isn't the time for it. Please help me, Mr. Roberts."

It would have been a far less impressionable man than the detective who could have refused the pleading glance of those pansy-blue eyes.

"How can I help you, Miss Vernon?"

"This way. Tell me of some detective, some really great one, who can unravel this tangle. I didn't kill Mr. Stannard. Barry didn't, either. But he says he did, to save me. Now, I want some one who can find the real criminal and so clear both Barry and myself."

"And you expect me to recommend somebody?"

"Oh, I do, Mr. Roberts, I do. I know you're big enough and honest enough to admit that you are at the end of your rope, and if you know of any one— I don't care how much he costs, I must have him— I must! Tell me, won't you?"

"Yes, I'll tell you, because I can't refuse you, but also because I know he will only verify our conclusions. You must know, Miss Vernon, we've had our eye on young Stannard all the time."

"Oh, I thought you were sure the criminal must be Mrs. Stannard or myself."

"We did think that at first—you see, we have to think what the evidence shows."

"Well, never mind that now. Who is this man you have in mind?"

"Alan Ford. He's not one of the story-book wizards, but he's a big light in the detective field, and he can find out if any one can."

"Where is he?"

Bobsy gave her the New York address of the detective, and Natalie rose to go. Then, acting on a sudden impulse, "Come with me," she said.

"To New York?" cried the amazed Bobsy.

"Yes. It's only a couple of hours' run, and I don't want to go alone."

"Why, I'm glad to go, if I can arrange it."

"Do arrange it. I want you so much."

Now, when a little flower-faced girl looks pleadingly out of heavenly colored eyes, and her red mouth quivers with fear of being refused, few men have the power to say no. Anyway, Bobsy hadn't, and he managed to "arrange" it, and in a few moments they were on their way.

"I thought you'd want to see Stannard," he said.

"No, I'd rather not, until I see if I can get the great Mr. Ford."

The little car ate up the miles, and soon they were in the crowded streets of the city.

Alan Ford was in his office, and received them with his characteristic quiet dignity.

The tall, big man looked taller than ever as he stood beside the petite model, his grey eyes looking down into her eager blue ones.

"What can I do for you?" he asked, kindly, and smiled at her because he couldn't help it. The winsome face made everybody smile from sheer gladness of looking at it.

"Can you take a case, Mr. Ford? An important murder case?"

"The Stannard case?"

"Yes."

"I'd like to say yes, but I am just starting on a Western trip, and I shall be gone at least a month."

Great crystal tears formed in Natalie's eyes and one rolled down her cheek. She couldn't possibly help this, the teardrops were beyond her control. But they stood her in good stead, for Alan Ford couldn't bear to see a woman cry. It unnerved him as no danger or terror could do.

"Don't, please," he said, impulsively.

"But I'm so disappointed! You see Barry Stannard has confessed—"

"What! Young Stannard confessed! Then what do you want of me?"

"Because Barry didn't do it. He confessed to save me."

"And did you do it?" The question was in the tone of a casual every-day inquiry, but few people would have replied anything but the truth with Alan Ford's gaze upon them.

"No, I didn't. You must come up there and find out who did do it. Oh, can't you manage somehow?"

The coaxing face was brightened by a sudden hope, and Alan Ford couldn't bring himself to dash that hope from the lovely beseeching girl.

"It makes a difference, now that they've arrested Stannard," he said, slowly.

"Oh, of course it does! Arrested him wrongfully, too. You see, he had to say he did it, or I would have been arrested."

"Tell me the main facts," said Ford to Bobsy. And in straightforward terms, Bobsy told the great detective all that the force had been able to accomplish.

"It would seem," said Alan Ford, speaking with deliberation, "that the criminal must be one of the four people most nearly connected with the dead man. His wife, Miss Vernon here, Barry, the son, or Mr. Courtenay, the lover."

"I don't like for you to use that term," said Natalie, gently. "For Mr. Courtenay and Mrs. Stannard could not be called lovers during Mr. Stannard's life."

"Good for you, for standing up for her. Well, I will postpone my Western trip for a few days at least."

"He's coming," said Natalie, briefly, as in the late afternoon she arrived at The Folly.

"Who is?" asked Joyce, "and where have you been?"

Joyce and Beatrice were having tea in the Reception Room, for by common consent all the household avoided the Studio.

The servants shuddered as they were obliged to pass it or go through it, and Natalie declared it was haunted.

"I've been to New York," the girl replied, as she flung off her motor coat, and threw herself into a big armchair. "Give me some tea, please, and I'll tell you all about it. I've engaged Alan Ford."

"Who is he?" asked Beatrice, fixing a cup of tea as Natalie liked it.

"He's a great, big, splendid detective—I mean big in his profession—and he's also the biggest man I ever saw, physically."

"Well, I am glad!" exclaimed Joyce. "I think Mr. Roberts has done all he could, but I don't think he has much real cleverness. Do you, Beatrice?"

"No. And yet, we oughtn't to judge him too harshly. He's had a hard time of it, for every new bit of evidence he gets, or thinks he gets, seems to point to some one of the family here."

"I know it," agreed Natalie, "but Alan Ford will find the real murderer and then we'll all be freed of suspicion."

"What's that, Natalie? Alan Ford!" And into the room strode Barry Stannard.

Natalie's face shone with welcome. "How did you get here?" she cried; "I thought you were arrested!"

"Even a murder suspect can get bail if he has money enough," said Barry, "and there were other reasons. They wouldn't swallow my confession whole. But never mind that now; tell me, did you say Alan Ford is coming?"

"I did, Barry, dear. I went and got him. And just in time, too, for he was going West at once. But he's staying over for us, and he's coming out here to-morrow morning. Isn't it fine!"

"Splendid! You're a trump, Natalie. You know, girl, don't you, why I confessed?"

"Of course I do. I was sure you couldn't make the police believe you, and then I knew it would swing back to me. So I had to take desperate measures, and I did."

"Barry," said Joyce, "your attempts to get suspicion turned your way, or any way, are too transparent. You scratched up the window frame to make it appear a burglar had entered there, and nobody believed it for a minute."

"I know it, I'm no good as a deceiver. But, oh, Natalie, don't think I suspected you, but I knew others would, and did, and I was frantic. And I vowed I did it, in an effort to distract their attention from you. But your going yourself for Ford, clears you in every one's eyes, and now he'll find the man. It was some man who came in—it has to be. There is no other explanation—positively none."

"It wasn't Eugene!" whispered Joyce, her face drawn with new apprehension.

"Of course it wasn't," said Beatrice, soothingly. "Don't worry over that, Joyce, dear. Mr. Wadsworth has exculpated Mr. Courtenay."

"But nothing seems sure," Joyce said, with a sad shake of her head.

"Well, it will be sure, once Alan Ford gets here," declared Barry. "I can hardly wait to see him."

Alan Ford arrived the next morning. When he 1 entered the Reception Room, his tall, commanding presence seemed to fill the whole room. With perfect courtesy, he greeted Joyce first, and then the others, and finally seated himself, facing the group.

Though not to be called handsome, his face was fine and scholarly, and his iron grey hair made him look older than his fifty years. His manner was quiet, but alert, as if no hint or lightest word could escape his attention.

"Let us waste no time," he began, "for my business engagements are pressing, and what I do here must be done as quickly as possible. I can promise you nothing, for the accounts I have read of this case make it seem to me that your local workers have done all that could be expected of them. The whole affair is mysterious, but sometimes a new point of view or the opinions of a different mind may lead to something of importance."

"You know the main details, then?" asked Barry.

"The main details as told in the papers, yes. Also, I've seen Mr. Roberts this morning, and I've discussed matters with him and with Captain Steele. But never mind those sources of information. I want the stories of each one of you here. And, if you please, I want them separately, and in each instance, alone. Otherwise, I cannot take the case."

"Why, of course, Mr. Ford," said Joyce, "we will agree to anything you stipulate. Please direct us, and we will obey."

"Then first, I will talk with Mr. Stannard, and later with the ladies. Also, I must ask that the interviews be in the Studio, the room where the crime took place. This is not only because it is more appropriate, but I can think better in a large room. This little low-ceiled box of a room doesn't give me space to think!"

Ford's winsome smile took all hint of rudeness from the words, and as he rose, his great height and proportionate bulk seemed to bear out his statement, and the assumption that his mind was of wide scope and far-reaching limits, made it seem plausible that he felt stifled in a small or low room.

"But you haven't yet been in the studio," said Natalie. "How do you know it is big and high?"

"It was so described in the newspaper accounts. That is why I took an interest in the case. Also, I am willing to admit, I paused for a glance in at the studio door, as I came into the house, and before I entered this room."

"A queer man," thought Natalie. "Why should a great detective talk about such foolish details as large or small rooms? Why should he take an interest in a case because of them?"

The others had similar thoughts, but no comment was made on the visitor's peculiarities, save that Beatrice Faulkner seemed to feel obliged to defend her husband's architectural ideas.

"The rooms are carefully proportioned," she said, pleasantly, but with a touch of pride in the fact. "The architect who designed them knew just what measurements were most effective from a technical and artistic point of view."

"The rooms are all right," said Mr. Ford, smiling kindly at the speaker, "the trouble is with my own foolish vagaries."

Then led by Barry, they all went into the studio.

Alan Ford looked around him, with the most intense admiration expressed on his fine face.

"Magnificent!" he said. "Mrs. Faulkner, your late husband was indeed a genius. I have never seen a more perfectly proportioned room, or one more appropriately and effectively decorated. The windows are marvels and the furniture is in every respect fitting."

"Oh," said Joyce, "Mr. Stannard furnished the room. It was not built for a studio."

"It is, then, the joint product of two geniuses. I know of Mr. Stannard's reputation."

For a few moments Alan Ford seem to forget the errand on which he had come. He was, it was plain to be seen, deeply impressed with the beautiful apartment, and his dark, deep-set grey eyes roved about from pictures to statues, from furniture to decorations with admiring and approving gaze.

"Have you a picture of Mr. Stannard?" he said at last.

"Yes," and Joyce took a photograph from a small chest full of portraits. "This is a photograph of a painting done by himself. It was made about four years ago, but he changed little since."

Ford took the card and studied it. He saw a noble head and brow, fine features, and a general air of self appreciation that was, however, not to be called conceit. The mouth had a few weak lines about its corners, but on the whole it was the presentment of a man of genius.

"Have you a photograph of the subject in life?" he asked; "not taken from a painting."

"Yes, but not a recent one," replied Joyce. "Except for some little snapshots," and she put a halfdozen small pictures in the hands of the detective.

"Better yet," Ford said, and he carefully scrutinized the papers.

But all the pictures of Eric Stannard gave the same impression of power, self-confidence and dominance.

CHAPTER 18: QUESTIONS AND ANSWERS

STILL studying the face of the artist, Alan Ford indicated his desire to begin the successive interviews with the members of the household. All but Barry left the room, and the young man sat down near the absorbed detective.

"Your father was a handsome man," Ford said, as he laid aside the pictures.

"Yes," agreed Barry. "I wish I might have been more nearly his type."

"Physically, you mean?"

"Yes, and mentally, too. I admit my father's moral weakness, yet he was not a bad man, as men go. His artistic temperament was responsible for his being blamed far more than was just or right."

"That is probably true," said Ford, seriously. "To a man of that sensitiveness to beauty many things seemed right that were not. Now, Mr. Stannard, will you please tell me everything about the actual facts as you know them, regarding the hour or half hour in which the crime was committed? Don't shade or colour your story to shield Miss Vernon, for such a bias will only prejudice my judgment against her. Tell me exactly the events as they followed one another to your positive knowledge, and nothing more."

"Very well, Mr. Ford, I will do just as you ask. But let me say this first; there are three suspects—"

"Excuse me, there are four suspects."

"If you count Mr. Courtenay, yes. But the three in the house, my stepmother, Miss Vernon and myself, have been definitely suspected and, probably, are still. So I want to say, that if one of us must remain under suspicion, let it be me. It is impossible that a woman did this deed. So investigate along the line of Courtenay or myself, but as I feel quite sure you can get no real evidence against him, use me for a scapegoat, while you are finding the real criminal."

"Then you are not the criminal, Mr. Stannard?"

"If I were, would I be apt to tell you?"

"You couldn't help telling me. Not in words, but in manner, in glance, in intonation, in a dozen ways, over which you have no control."

"Have I told you so?"

"You have not. I know positively you did not kill your father. But, go on, please, with your recital."

"Well, after dinner, Miss Vernon and I sat on the terrace "Barry paused. "By Jove," he

broke out, "how can I tell you the straight truth? It sounds exactly as if Natalie did it!"

Alan Ford almost smiled at the boy's impetuous exclamation, but merely prompted him, "Yes. Go right on, remember the truth will help Miss Vernon more than any falsehood possibly could. Have you never heard of seemingly incriminatory evidence of one leading straight to another?"

"All right, then. We sat there a long time, and then we talked about—about getting married. I was bothered about it, for Dad had vowed if I married Natalie, he'd cut me out of his will."

"That's why you altered the will in Miss Vernon's favour?"

"I didn't alter that will! This is man to man, now, Mr. Ford. I'm telling you the truth. I didn't change that will, and Miss Vernon didn't, either. I don't know who did."

"We'll find that out. It won't be a great surprise to learn the truth about that."

"How do you know it won't? Do you know who did the forgery?"

"I think so. Or perhaps there wasn't any forgery. But go on, my dear boy, with your story. I told you, you know, I've not much time to give you."

"All right. We talked about getting married, and I got awful mad and I said if Father didn't stop his nonsense with her, I'd kidnap her and run away. And Natalie knew that if we did that, Dad would cut us both out of his will,—and she isn't a bit mercenary, it wasn't that."

"What was it, then?"

"Why, only that we're—why, hang it all, decent people don't do those things."

"Decent people don't commit murder, either," said Ford, very gravely.

"No, I know that. Well, Natalie begged me not to quarrel with father,—said she could manage him herself. And I thought she meant by being sweet to him, and all that, and I got mad at her, and—I walked off and left her there."

"Without a word?"

"No. I told her I was going to give the dogs a run. I was going to, too, but as I walked away, I fell a-thinking, and I just strolled round the place alone."

"Whom did you see?"

"Nobody at all. Maybe Courtenay or Mr. Wadsworth or some of those people passed me, I don't know. I was just thinking about Natalie, and then Halpin came running out and told me to come in the house, my father was ill."

"And you went right in?"

"Yes, and when I saw what had happened, I felt afraid Natalie had killed him—and I ran out and tried to make the window frame look as if a burglar had broken in. I suppose it was foolish."

"It certainly was. But I don't blame you. It was natural to try to shield the girl you loved from possible suspicion."

"Possible suspicion! If you had seen the situation! There were the two women, both shivering with fear and terror, and there was the dead or dying man between them! Why, Mr. Ford, it wasn't suspicion, it was certainty that one or the other had stabbed him!"

"And why have you changed your mind since?"

"Partly because of that clairvoyant person. I don't believe in those things, but—well—do you?"

"I do not. But I can see how she would turn suspicion away from the two women in question. Who sent for the clairvoyant?"

"Mrs. Stannard did, but, first, the Priestess, as she likes to be called, wrote and asked for a seance."

"She did! How did she know she was wanted?"

"She didn't know. Said she read about the case, and got interested."

"Ah, a professional medium."

"She said not. Said she only offers to help in cases that appeal especially to her."

"H'm. Well, then she turned all your thoughts toward Mr. Courtenay, I am told."

"But she didn't intend to. I mean, she described a man who entered the room, and who stabbed my father, but it was Bobsy Roberts' questions that made anybody think of Eugene Courtenay?"

"How?"

"Oh, he kept saying, Bobsy did, 'Has he a pointed beard?' and 'is he tall and dark?' and such leading hints. The woman said 'Yes' every time, but I don't believe she knew what she was talking about."

"And her mysterious reading of those sealed papers? You see, I know all the main facts, I just want your opinions."

"Well, you've got me there! That woman had to read those by supernatural power, because there's no other explanation. I know a bit about legerdemain and parlour magic and there was no opportunity whatever for any trickery. We wrote the things, sealed them, Bobsy Roberts collected them and handed them to her. Then in the same instant he switched off the light, and it wasn't half a minute before she was reading them aloud to us."

"In the dark?"

"Absolutely dark. And she hadn't moved from her chair, for her voice came from the place she was sitting."

"Ventriloquism?"

"Oh, no. Not a chance. Anyway, where could she go to have a light? The studio doors were all closed, and—why, of course, she didn't leave her chair, for when Bobsy switched on the light, suddenly, there she sat, eyes closed, hands quiet, composed and unruffled. No, sir, there's no explanation for that reading business but honest-to-goodness second sight! And, she gave us back our envelopes intact, seals unbroken."

"Well, but, Mr. Stannard, if she had power to do all that, and I don't doubt your word in the least particular, isn't it strange that she couldn't see exactly who that murderer was?"

"Suppose it was some one she didn't know?"

"But oughtn't her powers of second sight, if she has such, reveal to her the identity of the man? She didn't know what was in your envelopes, but she told you. Why didn't her supernatural powers inform her the man's name?"

"I don't know, Mr. Ford. I'm only telling you what I saw and heard."

"That's all I want." And after a short further conversation, Alan Ford dismissed Barry and asked Mrs. Stannard to come to him next.

"It will be hard for you, I know," he said gently, as he placed a chair for her, "but I want you to tell me just what occurred at the time of Mr. Stannard's death. Tell only your own part, only what you, yourself, did or saw."

"You suspect I killed my husband?" said Joyce, in a choking whisper.

"It will depend on your story, what I suspect. Do not be afraid and do not distrust me, Mrs. Stannard. I want to help you, in any case. Whatever the truth, I can help you, and I want to assure you of that."

The infinite gentleness of his tone, the kind light in his eyes and the utter sympathy evident in his whole manner reassured Joyce, and in a low voice she began.

"I have told it so many times, I know it by heart. I was in the Billiard Room with Mr. Courtenay. I will not explain or defend the fact that I was there alone with him, but merely state that I was. He left me, and as I was heartsick over my own private and personal affairs, I buried my head in a sofacushion and cried. Not a real crying spell of sobs and tears, but an emotion which I endeavoured to restrain or control that I might meet others without causing comment. As I bowed my head there, I am positive I heard my husband talking to some woman."

"Miss Vernon?"

"I thought so at first, now I am not sure it was she."

"Mrs. Faulkner?"

"Oh, no. She was in the drawing-room at the other end of the house. No, it must have been either my imagination or some woman who had somehow entered and who afterward disappeared."

"Go on."

"I heard him say, or I thought I did, that she could have the emeralds, but he refused to marry her."

"Yes," a little impatiently. "I know about that. Tell me what happened."

"Then I heard a strange, gasping sound, and I rushed in—"

"Was the room light then?"

"No, dark. The light went out that instant or a moment before. I pushed in, and I heard a sound opposite—on the other side of the room. At first, I thought it was my husband, but it was a quick, frightened breathing, and then the light flashed on and I saw it was Miss Vernon, huddled against the wall—no, against a small table, and looking scared to death. Do you wonder that I thought she had done something wrong? For just then I caught sight of my husband, stabbed, dying—oh, I knew in that first glance that he had been murdered. Then, I saw Blake and Mrs. Faulkner at the other end of the room. They were shocked and frightened, too, but I paid no attention to them, I looked right back to Eric. And he—well, the footman did ask him who did it—and he raised his hand and said 'Neither Natalie nor Joyce.'"

"Are you sure that's what he said?"

"I am sure now. At the time he said it, he spoke so thickly I could scarcely understand him, and I thought he said 'Natalie, not Joyce.' But we had a clairvoyant here, and she said he said 'nor' and then I realized at once that that was what he did say!"

"Meaning, of course, that you two women were innocent, and that some other hand had struck the blow?"

"Yes, that was what he meant."

"And, do you not think, Mrs. Stannard, that he would have said that to shield you both, even if one had been guilty?"

Joyce Stannard turned white. "I—I never thought of that," she stammered. "Perhaps he would."

"But you feel sure, at this moment, that it was not Miss Vernon who killed your husband?"

Joyce looked utterly miserable. Her eyes were frightened like those of a hunted animal. But she said, bravely, "I feel sure of that, Mr. Ford. Miss Vernon is not one who could do such a thing."

"She doesn't seem to be. Will you go now, Mrs. Stannard, and please send Miss Vernon in here?"

Joyce went slowly out of the studio, and in a moment Natalie Vernon came in.

"Am I afraid of you?" she asked, as she sat facing Alan Ford. "Need I be?"

Her questions were not prompted by coquetry, that was evident. Her tone was serious, and she looked at the detective wistfully.

"No, Miss Vernon," he answered, seriously, "you have no reason to be afraid of me, but I will tell you frankly, you have great reason to fear the consequences if you tell me anything but the exact truth. Pardon me, if that seems a rude speech, but great issues are at stake and prevarication on your part to the slightest degree would baffle all my plans and hopes."

"I will tell the truth," Natalie sighed, "so far as I know it. But sometimes it's very hard to be sure of what is true."

"Yes, I know it. Now, Miss Vernon, just one word about the time and scene of the crime. When you came into the studio, because you heard—what did you hear?"

Alan Ford's manner was calculated to set the nervous girl at her ease, and his kindliness made her calm and un-self-conscious.

"I heard Eric moan."

"Did you know at once it was Mr. Stannard?"

"Oh, yes. It sounded like him, and I suppose he was in there."

"What did you think ailed him?"

"I don't believe I thought of that. I just heard the curious gasping sound, as of somebody choking, and I ran in. I didn't think,—I only wondered what was the trouble."

"And when you entered the room was it light or dark?"

"Honestly, I don't know, Mr. Ford. I've been so quizzed and questioned about it, that I can't seem to remember clearly."

"But the lights went out?"

"Yes, just as I entered, or a minute before."

"Well, then, what was the first thing you saw?"

"Must I tell that?"

"Yes, and truly."

"Then, the first thing I saw, as the light flashed on,—and it rather blinded me at first, you know. You see, I had been sitting on the Terrace, which was almost dark, then I entered the dark room, and so when the light came suddenly, it dazzled me, and I naturally looked straight ahead of me. I saw Mrs. Stannard, behind her husband, and near the Billiard Room door."

"As if she had just come in from that room?"

"I think so,—now. I didn't think so then. I thought she had killed him, and had sort of stepped back, you know—"

"Why did you change your mind?"

"Oh, because of Madame Orienta. Haven't you heard about her? She cleared up the mystery as far as Joyce,— Mrs. Stannard and I are concerned."

"Yes, I've heard all about her. You believe in her supernatural powers?"

"Oh, yes. Only I don't use that word. I call them psychic powers."

"But it was supernatural to read the sealed messages as she did?"

"Well, I suppose it was. I suppose clairvoyance is supernatural, but we psychics prefer other terms. You know I'm a psychic."

"Ah, is that so? And you can read sealed messages in the dark?"

"No, indeed, I can't. I wish I could. But perhaps I shall be able to some day. I can—Mr. Ford, you believe me, don't you?"

Natalie looked at him, and a slight flush came to her pale cheek as she saw his slightly quizzical expression.

"Miss Vernon, I believe all you've said, so far. I want to continue my confidence in your statements, so please be very careful not to exaggerate or over-colour the least mite. Now, just to what extent do you know you're a psychic? Not imagine or hope or think, but know."

"Well, I only know that I've heard the voice of Mr. Stannard's spirit since his death, as clearly as I heard his mortal voice that night he died."

"You are sure of this?"

"I am sure, Mr. Ford."

"Tell me the exact circumstances."

CHAPTER 19: FORD'S DAY

MRS. STANNARD and I were alone, here in the studio—"

"Where was Mr. Stannard?"

"I don't know. He wasn't in the house."

"Was Mrs. Faulkner?"

"Yes, but she wouldn't stay here with us. She doesn't approve of any of these psychic investigations, but she doesn't say much against them, out of respect to Mrs. Stannard's and my wishes."

"Go on."

Natalie told the story of hearing faint groans, as of a dying man, and of the sudden extinguishing of the lights.

"One moment, Miss Vernon. When the lights went out, the room was quite still, was it not?"

"Deathly silent, Mr. Ford. Joyce and I were breathless, listening for further sounds of any sort."

"And, tell me, did you hear the click of the switch as the light went out?"

"Yes, I did. I heard it distinctly."

"And did that mean nothing to you?"

"Why, what could it mean?"

"It meant, Miss Vernon, that the light was switched off by a mortal,—flesh and blood hand. Had it been supernaturally extinguished there would have been no sound."

"I heard it,—I'm sure I heard it. But I think the spirit of Mr. Stannard haunts the whole room, and it was he who turned the light off."

"By means of a material switch?"

Natalie looked a little uncertain. Varying expressions passed over her face as she thought it out. Then she said, "Don't spirits ever use material means?"

"Not to my individual knowledge," returned Alan Ford gravely. "I fear, Miss Vernon, your belief in the spiritual influences at work in this affair is about to be rudely shattered. Now, did you hear any other sound,—a click or thud,—after the light went out?"

"No. You see, Joyce,—Mrs. Stannard jumped right up and ran across the room and turned on the light."

"Turned it on? It had been really turned off, then?"

"Oh, yes. And she turned it on. Then she opened the door and Blake was in the hall, where he belonged. He had seen no one and had heard nothing."

"I must have a chat with Blake. And Mrs. Faulkner, she knew nothing of it all?"

"Not till Mrs. Stannard told her. She ran at once to Mrs. Faulkner's room—"

"Where is that room?"

"At the other end of the house, on the third floor. And there she found Mrs. Faulkner writing letters. And Mrs. Stannard told her and they came down stairs together. Well, and after Mrs. Stannard left the room, of course, I looked around, and there was the case of jewels on the table."

"Where did they come from? How did they get there?"

"The spirit of Mr. Stannard placed them there," said Natalie, solemnly. "You may scoff, Mr. Ford, you may suspect Blake of being mixed up in it, but you're all wrong. The studio doors were locked—"

"While you and Mrs. Stannard were in there?"

"Yes, I locked them myself. All three. There are but three, you know. See, the one to the front hall, the outside one to the Terrace and the one to the Billiard Room. I locked them, and the windows were fastened too. Nobody mortal could have come into that room."

"So it would seem. Now, who else has these leanings toward spirit forces beside you? Who sent for the clairvoyant lady?"

"Nobody. That is, she wrote herself to Mrs. Stannard, asking if she might come."

"You liked her? You believed in her?"

"In Orienta? Oh, yes. She is not an ordinary person,— I mean she is refined, educated, cultured, —as correct in every way as we are ourselves. She's not a professional medium, you know."

"I know. And did Mr. Barry Stannard want her to come?"

"No; he strongly opposed it."

"And Mrs. Faulkner?"

"She deferred to Mrs. Stannard's wishes. But she had no faith in her. Of course, after Orienta read the sealed letters, Mrs. Faulkner had to believe in that, she couldn't well help it."

"No. Now, Miss Vernon, when you heard the groan or sigh as if the spirit of Mr. Stannard were expressing itself, where did the sound come from?"

"It seemed to come from that chair,—the chair he died in. Joyce and I sat facing it—"

"Your backs to the hall door, then?"

"Yes, but nobody could open that door, it was locked. Mrs. Stannard unlocked it when she ran out of the room."

"You're sure of this?"

"Positive. We've gone over the scene a dozen times or more."

"That seems to let Blake out, doesn't it? Well, that's all for the present, Miss Vernon, and thank you for your courteous attention. Now, there's no one to interview but the servants."

"Mrs. Faulkner? She expects you to talk to her, I think."

"What could she tell me? She wasn't in this part of the house at the spiritual seance, and as to the moment of the crime, she tells no more than Blake. However, I'll see her for a brief interview. It's always well to get all the accounts possible."

Natalie left the studio, and in a few moments Beatrice Faulkner came in.

"Just a question or two, Mrs. Faulkner," said Ford, "I know you people are all nearly distraught with these strange and sudden developments. But, tell me, what do you think of Miss Vernon's story of the spirit manifestations in this room?"

"I think it was all the girl's imagination, Mr. Ford. She is not only of an exaggerated artistic temperament, but excessively nervous and susceptible to hallucinations."

"She is all that, I think. Now, please tell me, very honestly and very carefully, exactly how Mrs. Stannard looked and acted when she ran up to your room to tell you of the strange occurrence in the studio."

"She was terribly excited, Mr. Ford," and she could scarcely speak. She stumbled up the stairs—"

"Why, did you see her?"

"No, I heard her. I was at my writing desk, and the house was still. Then she flew into my room, without knocking—"

"Is it her custom to knock?"

"Oh, yes, she always does. And she begged me to go down stairs with her, and I did. The rest you know?"

"Yes, and a strange tale it is. How do you suppose the jewels came to be on that table?"

"I cannot say," Beatrice looked sad. "There seems to be only one explanation. That whoever had them or knew where they were, placed them there."

"And how did the bearer of the box get into the locked room?"

"I can't imagine. The only thing I can think of is that Natalie didn't lock the door as thoroughly as she thinks she did."

"Mrs. Faulkner, tell me this. I assure you I will not use your information unless absolutely necessary. Do you suspect the footman Blake of any connivance—or of any wrong doing in the whole matter?"

Beatrice Faulkner hesitated. Then she said, "No, Mr. Ford, I do not. I think Blake a thoroughly honest and trustworthy servant."

"And who is the criminal?"

"That I cannot say. I am, as you know, merely a visitor, who chanced to be here at this unfortunate time. I have hesitated to express my opinions lest I do harm to the innocent or retard the quest of the guilty. I can only answer your questions in so far as they are not leading up to suspicion of any of my friends."

"That is the right attitude, Mrs. Faulkner. I thought there was no necessity for troubling you at all, but one or two minor points I prefer to ask of you rather than Mrs. Stannard. Do you know the identity of 'Goldenheart'?"

"I imagine her to be one of Mr. Stannard's early inamoratas. He had many, and, moreover, I should not be surprised to learn that he called more than one by that name. You know there was a small gift found in his desk addressed to some one of that name, which had never been sent. It has occurred to me that the Goldenheart of that matter, and the one to whom he wrote more recently, were not the same person."

"That may well be. You have a logical mind, Mrs. Faulkner. I say this to you, because I want your help. If I should tell you that I do not suspect Mrs. Stannard or Miss Vernon or Barry Stannard, would you then be willing to assist me in my investigation?"

Beatrice Faulkner looked at the detective an instant, and then said, in a low tone, "Mr. Courtenay?"

"Hush! Don't mention names. Let us close this conversation right here, and I will tell you at some other time what I want you to do for me."

Beatrice went away, and locking the door after her exit, Alan Ford remained alone in the studio for an hour or more.

Then he went for a walk which lasted another hour, and when he joined the family at luncheon, he was merely a courteous, friendly guest, with no suggestion of a detective.

In the afternoon, he requested permission to go over all of Eric Stannard's papers and correspondence and spent his time until dusk at this work.

At tea time, he rejoined the others, and during the tea hour he talked of the visit of Orienta and her wonderful performance. Over and over it was discussed, and at each fresh detail or opinion Alan Ford grew more and more interested.

"Tell me of her costume," he said, at last, when it seemed he had heard about every other bit of possible interest.

"It was beautiful!" exclaimed Natalie. "A long, full robe of a sort of sage green—"

"What material?" asked Ford, and Barry looked at him in surprise. What kind of a great detective was this who inquired concerning the texture of a costume?

"Why, it was silk, I think,—yes, heavy silk, wasn't it, Joyce?"

"That, or a silk poplin. It was not a modern, modish gown at all; it was like a draped shawl."

"Drapery hanging from the shoulders?"

"Yes," Natalie answered, her mind so intent on giving Ford the right idea, that she didn't think of the queerness of the question.

"Double skirt?"

"Yes—or, that is, a skirt, and then an over drapery in full long folds. Oh, it was lovely!"

"Are you apt with your pencil, Miss Vernon? Could you draw a rough sketch of that gown?"

"I can't but Mrs. Faulkner can. She's good at sketching draperies. Here's a paper pad, Beatrice. Will you draw it for Mr. Ford?"

"Certainly," and taking the paper, Beatrice rapidly sketched an indication of Orienta, in her flowing robe.

"That's just right," said Natalie, "but the folds were fuller, I think."

"Never mind," said Ford, "this will do. I only wanted to get a mental picture of how she looked," and tearing the picture into strips he tossed them into a waste basket.

The talk drifted to the house and its architecture.

"The whole house is a gem," said Alan Ford, enthusiastically, "but the staircase is a marvel. Nowhere in this country have I seen its equal. Your husband studied abroad, Mrs. Faulkner?"

"For years. He took great pride in building this house, as he intended it to be a masterpiece."

"Which it certainly is. Have you the plans of it? I should like to see them. Architecture is one of my hobbies."

"No, I haven't the plans, Mr. Ford."

"Oh, of course, they went to Mr. Stannard with the title deeds. Have you them, Mrs. Stannard?"

"No, we never had them. I never thought about them."

"Doubtless they are among Mr. Stannard's belongings. They must have been given to him. It doesn't matter. I oughtn't to take time to look at them, anyway. But one thing I do want to see, and that is the picture of Mrs. Faulkner that Mr. Stannard was engaged on at the time of his death. I'm told it is an example of his best work. May I have a glimpse of it?"

Beatrice Faulkner looked a little flattered at this request, but she said only, "Certainly, Mr. Ford. It is in the studio."

They all went in to see it, and Barry arranged the portrait on an easel and adjusted a light for it .

"It is indeed splendid," said Ford, in genuine admiration. The portrait was excellent and lifelike, but more than that it was a work of art. Beatrice, in a gown of deep ruby velvet, with the great staircase for a background, was at her very best. Her face, always handsome, was imbued with a fine spiritual grace, and she looked the embodiment of happiness. The whole conception was, perhaps, a little idealised, but it was a magnificent portrait, and a stunning picture.

"I'm so glad you have it, Beatrice," said Joyce, softly. "You've been so good and dear, and have done so much for us all ever since Eric's death, I'm happy for you to have this remembrance of him."

"I'm glad, too," and Beatrice looked at the reflection of herself through misty eyes.

Bobsy Roberts came in while they were looking at the portrait, and he, too, was charmed with its beauty.

"That staircase makes a wonderful setting. I'm a fancier of staircases, and I think this one beats any I ever saw."

"A fancier of staircases, what do you mean?" asked Natalie.

"Yes, I've studied architecture, more or less, but the stairs have always especially interested me. I've just run across an old book, called 'Staircases and Steps,' and it's most interesting."

"I agree with you," said Alan Ford. "And the staircase here is a gem. That's why I wanted to see the plans of the house."

"Mayn't we see them?" asked Bobsy, turning to Joyce.

"Why, I haven't them, Mr. Roberts. Perhaps they're among my husband's belongings, but I've never seen them."

"You see," observed Ford, stepping out into the hall, "it's the wonderful proportion of one part to another that makes the beauty of it. The stairwell, clear to the roof, the arcaded hall, the noble high-ceiled studio and this little low-ceiled Reception Room, fitted in just here, make up a splendid whole. Did not your late husband feel this?" Ford added, turning to Beatrice.

"Yes," she replied, briefly, and then Bobsy tore himself away from the fascinating subject of architecture to ask Alan Ford if he had made any progress in his investigations.

"I have," replied Ford. "I have found out a lot of things that seem to me indicative. But it all hinges on whether there are spiritual influences at work or not. It seems to me, if the spirit of Mr. Stannard could return to earth and manifest itself in any way, it would prove—"

"Prove what?" asked Mrs. Faulkner, as the detective paused.

"Well, I may be foolish, but it would seem to me to prove that he wanted us to stop these investigations and let the matter remain a mystery."

"You really think that!" exclaimed Bobsy, as his estimation of Alan Ford's genius for detective work received a sudden setback.

"I think I agree with Mr. Ford," said Beatrice, thoughtfully. "If Eric wanted us to continue our inquiries he would rest quiet in his grave."

"Oh, Mr. Ford," and Natalie gave a little gasp, "do you really think, then, it was Mr. Stannard's spirit that I heard in the studio? Do you think I am enough of a sensitive to bring about a real manifestation?"

"Those things are hard to tell, Miss Vernon. But I am going to ask the privilege of spending to-night alone in the studio. Then if any demonstration occurs, I shall, as I told you, think there is reason to believe—"

Ford's pause was eloquent of deep feeling. Truly the man was in earnest, whether he was right or not.

"May I not stay there with you?" asked Roberts, a little diffidently.

"No, please. I want to be alone. I shall lock myself in, and I must ask not to be disturbed in any way."

"I wish I could stay with you," and Natalie sighed. "But I suppose you wouldn't want me to."

"No, please," said Ford, gently. "I must be alone."

CHAPTER 20: ON THE STAIRCASE

AT Ford's request, the evening was spent without reference to the matter that was uppermost in every mind. At dinner the detective was merely a pleasant and entertaining guest. Afterward, in the Drawing Room he proved himself a good talker and a good listener, and the conversation, on all sorts of topics, was casual and interesting.

It was nearly midnight when Ford bade them good night, and went to the studio to hold his vigil. The others followed him in, Joyce asking if he would like any refreshment served during the night.

"No," he replied. "It will not be so very long until daylight. And, too, perhaps nothing will happen, and I may fall asleep. Don't worry about me, Mrs. Stannard, I shall not be at all uncomfortable. See, I shall sit just where Miss Vernon sat the other night. Right here, facing the chair in which Mr. Stannard died. Thus, I have my back to the hall door, and the North window, but I shall make sure that all are securely locked, and then if any manifestation occurs, I shall have every reason to be sure it is of supernatural origin."

"And that would make you give up the case?" asked Beatrice, incredulously.

"I think so," returned Ford. "I should probably leave here to-morrow."

"Well, of all queer detectives!" said Barry Stannard, as they went from the room and heard the click of the key as it was turned in the door behind them.

True to his word, Alan Ford examined with minutest care every door and window. He made sure no lock or catch was left unfastened, and then, the lights burning brightly, he took his seat just where he had said he would, facing the chair in which Eric Stannard had met his fate. Also, he faced the two doors that led respectively to the Billiard Room and the Terrace. This left more than half the room behind him and out of his line of vision. But the detective paid no attention to that part of the studio, and rested his contemplative gaze on the great armchair which had helped to stage the tragedy.

The hours went by. Alan Ford scarcely moved from the easy, relaxed position he had taken at first. He closed his eyes for the most of the time, now and then slowly opening them for a moment.

His left hand, lying on his knee, clasped some small object.

It was shortly after three o'clock in the morning, when there was the sound of a click and the lights went out.

The studio was in absolute darkness.

Ford rose quickly and crossed the room to the light switch by the hall door. He knew the position of the furniture, and felt his way by the chairs. As he did so, he heard a long, gasping sigh, and a faint cry of "Help!"

By this time he had reached the switch and turned it on. The sudden flash of light showed no one in the room save himself, but not pausing to look about, he unlocked the hall door, passed quickly through and ran up the first steps of the stairs.

On he went to the second great square landing, and there he paused. He did not stand still, but stepped about on the landing, making exclamations to himself, and breathing heavily. He leaned against the baluster, tapping on the newel post with his fingers. Then, he sat down on the lowest step of the third or upper division of the flight. He sat, tapping his foot against the stair, he even whistled a little under his breath. He seemed anxious not to be silent.

There was a low light in all the halls, and occasionally Ford leaned his head over the baluster and commanded a view of the hall below.

Half an hour passed, and then Joyce Stannard appeared from the hall above. She wore a boudoir gown and slippers, and her weary eyes betokened a sleepless night. .

She started with surprise at sight of Alan Ford on the stairs. But he made a motion requesting her to be silent, and taking a bit of paper from his pocket he wrote:

"Say no word. Go back to the hall above and remain there, but out of sight of this spot, until I summon you. Overhear all you can, but on no account let yourself be seen."

Joyce read the strange message, and going back up the few steps she had descended, she sat on a hall window seat, concealed by a light curtain.

Then Alan Ford, with a short, sad sigh, stood up and approached the panelled wall of the staircase. Down the flights the panels of course slanted, but on the landing they were in level row.

Placing his lips to the wall itself, Ford said in a clear low whisper, "Will you come out?"

From behind the wall he heard an agonised moan.

"It would be better," he said, gently. "Do come."

Another moment passed, and then, a panel of the wainscot slid open and Beatrice Faulkner stepped forth onto the landing.

"You know all?" she said, and her great despairing eyes looked into those of the detective.

"Almost all," he returned, and his glance at her was infinitely sad. "You killed Stannard?"

"Yes," she said, and swayed as if she would fall to the floor.

Ford assisted her to stand and then gently aided her to a seat on the stair where he had sat a moment since.

Beatrice sank to the step and Ford closed the panel she had left open. He did not look into the place to which the panel gave entrance, for he knew what it was. It was the space above the Reception Room. He had seen when he entered the house that since the Reception Room and the studio were next each other and yet there was five or six feet difference in the height of their respective ceilings, that space must be a sort of loft or waste room. It showed from none of the sides. Both hall and studio were high ceiled. The staircase well reached to the roof. There was no explanation of the discrepancy but a waste space the size of the Reception Room and about six feet in height.

This space, of course, abutted on the studio, the hall, the stairs, and, on the other side, the outer or Terrace wall.

In the studio the balcony ran along the wall at about the height of the stair landing on the other side. Ford guessed at once that ingress to that waste space must be had from the studio or the stair landing or both. He now was sure that panels from both opened into it.

As he closed the panel, he noted that there was no secret or concealed fastening. Merely an ordinary flush spring catch, inconspicuous but not hidden.

Ford turned to the woman on the stairs. He sat down beside her. "Tell me about it," he said, and his voice was so gentle, his face so sad, that Beatrice turned to him as to a friend.

"There is little to tell," she said, wearily. "It is the story of a great love, a love too big and strong to be conquered by a weak-willed woman. I tried —oh, I tried— "

"Don't give way, Mrs. Faulkner, just tell me the main facts. You knew Mr. Stannard years ago?"

"I was his first love. We were schoolmates. I always loved him—more than loved him. I worshipped, adored him. He loved me,—but he was always fickle. He loved every woman he, saw. Then,—he married—his first wife, I mean, and I thought I should die. But never mind the past. I married, and I tried to forget Eric. My husband built this beautiful home, but he had financial troubles and couldn't keep it. Eric Stannard bought it, and meanwhile his wife had died, and he married my friend

Joyce. I tried to be reconciled, but the demon of jealousy tore my very heart out. I gave over this house to them and went away. A portrait of myself was to be part of the purchase price, and —even though I knew it would be acute torment to see Eric happy here with Joyce, I came to stay a month and have the picture painted. As I feared, the necessarily intimate association between the artist and myself quickened my never-dying love for him, until I was almost frantic. I could have stood it, though, had it been only his wife. But when he fell desperately in love with the model, I resented it for Joyce and myself both. But I had no thought of killing him,—don't think that!"

"It was done on a sudden impulse, then." Ford was watching her closely. He knew that her enforced calm might give way at any instant and he strove to speak quietly and lead her gently on to a confession. Moreover, he trusted that Joyce was listening, as he had asked her to do. Thus the confession would be witnessed.

"It was this way," and Beatrice looked piteously into his kind eyes. "Mr. Wadsworth asked me that night to marry him. We were in the drawing room, as you know. I wouldn't say yes, for I still had a faint hope of winning Eric. It was absurd for me to think it, but I was desperate. After Mr. Wadsworth left me, I sat a moment in the drawing room, and then I resolved to go to Eric, by the secret passage, of which only he and I knew, and beg him to put Joyce away and take me. I say this without shame, for I was—and am, still, so madly in love with him, that I had no shame regarding it, and would have suffered any ignominy or humiliation to win him. I went through that small space; it is not really secret, but no one has ever noticed it, and I went through to the studio, and stepping in the room, on the little balcony, I saw Eric below me, gazing at the etching of Natalie with an adoring look. He bent down and kissed the picture, and then I descended the stairs and spoke to him. I told him that Natalie loved Barry and hated him. I urged him to divorce Joyce and let her marry Eugene Courtenay and I begged him to marry me. He laughed at me! I shall never forget that laugh! But that wasn't why I killed him. It was because he turned again to that picture of Natalie and into his face came a look that I had never seen there. A look of love such as I had never been able to call forth on his face, a worshipping passion that transcended all love I had ever dreamed of. And that he felt for a little girl who hated him. Jealousy maddened me, and snatching up an etching tool I marred the wax beyond recognition. He turned on me, his face livid with rage. The contrast, —the look of love he had for the girl, the look of venomous hate he gave me, bereft me of my senses. No, I do not mean I did not know what I was doing,—I did know. I fully meant at that moment to kill him, and then to kill myself, that we might at least die together. I should not have thought of killing him if I hadn't chanced to have that tool in my hand. Nor should I have wanted to kill him but for his scorn of me and his love for her. The two together drove me wild, and I stabbed him in a moment of fierce passion that was love, not hate. Then, as I was about to draw forth the needle and stab myself, I saw that he was not dead. He looked at me, and I couldn't say it was with hatred. I think—I honestly think—that he gloried in my deed,—you cannot understand,— it is a strange idea, but I think he realised at last the depth of my love and appreciated it. Anyway, I read that in his face, and I couldn't bring myself to leave a world that still held him. I didn't dare remove the needle, lest it bring about his death,— I didn't dare remain and be found there with him. My mind fairly flew. I thought so fast and so clearly, I concluded to escape by the panel and return quickly through the hall and thus coming upon him, apparently innocently, save his life."

"You crossed the room," Ford prompted, for the speaker's strength was failing.

"Yes, I crossed the room, as deliberately as if nothing had happened. I turned off the light, that I might make good my escape. I flew through the panelled space, and in a few seconds I was out at this end, here on this landing and down the stairs. I saw at once that Blake had heard something, but whether it was a sound from Eric, or the noise of my departure I did not then know. I spoke to the man,—and the rest you know."

"You were surprised when the light was turned on to see the two women there?"

"I was dumfounded. I couldn't think at first what it would mean to me—or to them. I had no thought of allowing them to be suspected of the crime, but circumstances were too strong for me. They were found there, near the dying man,—I had, to all appearances come in from the other end of the room,—naturally they were suspected. And then reaction had come; no longer was I keyed up by that torment of jealousy, that spur of scorned love. I had time to think,—even when all were wondering and questioning, I had time to think. And I concluded I would never confess unless I was obliged to do so, to save some one else. I decided to devote every energy and use every effort to divert suspicion from all in the household. It was I who really arranged for—"

"For the clairvoyant," said Ford, as Beatrice paused from sheer weakness of breath.

"Yes, you understand that?"

"You hired her, instructed her to write to Mrs. Stannard, and you told her what to say."

"Yes, I wanted her to make it appear that the murderer was a man who had entered through the Billiard Room. I meant for the man's identity to be absolutely unknown. But they managed to fasten it on Mr. Courtenay and my plan failed utterly."

"And then?"

"Then I had about decided to tell the truth. When they arrested Barry, I quite decided. And then you came. I knew that was my death knell. But when you said if the spirit manifestation appeared in the studio to-night—that was a trap, wasn't it?"

"Yes, Mrs. Faulkner, it was a trap. I knew whoever had been playing 'spirit' by the use of the panelled space, would do it again to-night at my words, and I felt sure it would be you. I am sorry"

"I believe you are, Mr. Ford. I know from your whole attitude you are sorry for me. Otherwise, I could not have told you all this as I have done. You are more like a father confessor than a detective. It helps a little to know you are sorry for—"

"How did Orienta read the papers? The pocketlight method?"

"Yes. She is very clever; I've known her for years. She is not a medium at all. I persuaded her that to do as I asked would save innocent people from being suspected. Of course, she didn't know I was guilty."

"And you were 'Goldenheart'?"

"Yes. It was Eric's old pet name for me. He wrote that letter to me, giving me the emeralds if I would cease asking for his love. He said I knew where the jewels were, because he always kept them in the panelled space,— that's what we called it,— and Joyce did overhear him saying to me in the studio practically what he had written in the letter. Had she not been so wrapped up in her own heart trouble, she would have heard it clearly. Of course, too, that little golden heart that was bought and never presented was meant for me."

"You told Orienta to say that Mr. Stannard said 'Neither Natalie nor Joyce.'?"

"Yes, for I really think that was what he did mean to say. He wouldn't implicate me, even with his dying breath, but he tried to clear them. He was a wonderful man, Mr. Ford. Not a good man, perhaps, but a brave one. He would have defended any or all of us, but he had no chance. My love for him has been the mainspring of my whole life. Instead of forgetting him, I grew more madly in love with him year by year. I had no business to come here, and let him paint me. Those hours when I posed for him were the happiest I have ever known. That's why the portrait is of a happy woman. I hoped against hope that I could yet win him back. But I couldn't—I can only follow him."

The quietness of Beatrice's voice had lulled any suspicions Ford might have had of her intent, and when she drew from the folds of her bodice an etching needle, exactly like the one that had killed Eric, and drove it into her own breast, Ford wheeled suddenly and grasped her hand,—but too late. The deed was done.

At his exclamation, Joyce ran down from the hall above, where she had been listening to Beatrice's story. She sank down beside the wounded woman and took the drooping figure in her arms.

"Forgive—" moaned Beatrice. "Joyce,—forgive,—I—I loved him so."

"Yes,—yes," soothed Joyce, scarce knowing what she said. "What can we do, Mr. Ford? Oh, what can we do?"

"Nothing, I fear. Call help. Shall I ring?" Ford hastened to the nearest bell he could notice and rang it. Immediately people began to gather, servants, family,— and all sorts of contradictory orders were given. But with his finger on the pulse of the dying woman the detective tried to learn yet more facts. "The will," he asked, bending above her. "Who changed it?"

"Eric himself," Beatrice answered, "that's why —oh, Eric!" Her faced beamed with a strange radiance, and then sinking back in Joyce's arms, Beatrice Faulkner breathed her last.

The next day Alan Ford declared he must hasten away as his engagements were pressing.

"But tell us more of your work," implored Bobsy Roberts, "give us a few moments more."

"And tell us about that clairvoyant woman," said Barry. "If she was a fake, how did she read those papers in the dark?"

"I realised, before I came up here at all," said Ford, "that there had to be some secret means of entrance to the studio. I see now, it was never meant to be secret. The

architect made the Reception Room ceiling lower than the
studio ceiling, because it was a smaller room and he
observed due proportions. This left a space there, but it
was not concealed or hidden. The catches on both doors
are merely small ones and inconspicuous but not
concealed. Mr. Faulkner left all the house plans in that
loft and Eric Stannard knew of it. He chose to conceal his
jewels there as being a convenient place. Only he and
Mrs. Faulkner knew of the space, but that was merely a
chance happening. He, in no sense, kept it a secret. When
I read the accounts in New York papers I felt the case
must hinge on another entrance of some sort. When I
reached here I saw at once that there was a discrepancy
in the heights of those two ceilings, and I worked from
that. I was sure the spirit manifestations were made
possible by human means working through that
concealed space, and I found I was right. I assumed it was
probably Mrs. Faulkner who played the spirit as she
refused to show the plans of the house, and my theories,
based on those plans, left her free to do all she did do,
without being discovered. I found she could have placed
the jewels on the table that night and returned to her
room through the little loft, and be seated at her desk,
writing, when Mrs. Stannard reached her room. She said
she heard Mrs. Stannard coming up stairs, but as the
door was shut and the stairs thickly carpeted, this was
unlikely. So I assume she was expecting her. All facts
pointed to the guilt of Mrs. Faulkner, but they were by no
means obvious. So, when I said if spirits came to the
studio last night I should drop the case to-day, I meant
because it would be solved. But Mrs. Faulkner thought I
would give it up as unsolvable, so she played 'spirit'
again. I had in my hand a tiny mirror of the sort that
shows what is passing at one's back. I heard, as I sat
there, the soft opening of the panel in the studio balcony,
and I knew she was coming down the little stair. I heard
her click off the light, and just as she did so, I caught a
glimpse of her in my mirror. So I went out at the hall

door, snapping on the light as I passed, and went up on the grand staircase, knowing I would head her off, and have her practically penned in there. Mrs. Stannard found me waiting there, and I arranged for her to witness the confession that I knew must come. I did not foresee that Mrs. Faulkner would take her own life, but perhaps it is as well. There was no happiness or peace for her in this world, it was better she should expiate her own sin. Poor soul, she was a victim of a love that proved too great for her human nature to strive against. As to the will, I felt sure Mr. Stannard had made that change himself. It looked like his writing, and I felt sure neither Miss Vernon nor Mr. Barry Stannard would have done it."

"And you picked out the truth from the maze of probabilities and suspicion and false evidence—"

Bobsy looked at the great detective in an awed way.

"I gained most of my information and formed most of my conclusions from my talks with each one separately. I am a fairly good judge of character, and I saw at once neither Mrs. Stannard nor Miss Vernon was guilty. They were both uncertain and indefinite in their testimony. They scarcely knew even the sequence of events at the time of the tragedy; if they had been telling untruths, they would have been positive in their statements. Also, I saw at once Barry Stannard and Miss Vernon more than half feared each other guilty and each was ready for any sacrifice or effort to save the other. This let them both out, for neither could be guilty and suspect some one else! Mr. Courtenay had practically no real evidence against him, so it came back to Mrs. Faulkner. I talked to her enough to strengthen my suspicion in that direction and then tested her by the night in the studio. She proved herself the source of the 'spiritual' manifestations, and showed how she did it. That left only the matter of getting her confession. I feel deep pity for the poor woman; she led a sad, miserable existence because of a mistaken love. Also, I must admit that she was of a different stamp from the people here. Mrs. Faulkner was capable of strong passion that did not stop at crime. I judge the rest of you would not be, and I do not think I am mistaken in that."

Alan Ford looked around at the pure sweet face of Natalie, the noble countenance of Joyce, and the brave boyish frankness that shone in Barry's glance and sighed as he thought of the smouldering fires in the deep eyes of the woman who was conquered by her own evil passion.

"But tell us about the sealed reading," insisted Bobsy, as Ford rose to go.

"Oh, yes," cried Natalie, "how was that done?"

"One of the tricks of the trade," said Ford. "You know there are dozens of ways to read sealed writings."

"Yes, but what way did she use?"

"This way. You know, I insisted on a full description of her dress. When I found it was of full pattern and made of an opaque material, I understood. You see, if a message is written with ink, and if the paper is slipped, unfolded, into a moderately thin envelope, the writing can be read with ease in the dark by holding an electric pocket flashlight behind the envelope. Orienta, the room being darkened, drew the loose folds of her gown over her head, and thus shielded, took a little flashlight from her pocket, read them all, by its aid, then returning the light to her pocket, remembered the questions and spoke them out, both with and without a light. The second time, I believe, she read the first ones in the dark and the others in the light. There were no signatures, but she had learned each one's hand-writing from the first lot. The thing is simple, and is the most mystifying of all sealed paper readings."

"Will it always work?" asked Roberts, greatly interested.

"In total darkness, yes. Go into a dark closet and try it. Of course, Orienta's drapery served to aid her and also to conceal the light from her audience."

"And all the answers she made up,—or Beatrice had told her," said Natalie, thoughtfully.

"Yes," said Ford. "And now I must go. I shall hope to meet you all again some day, and if I can tell you anything more you care to learn about these make-believe wizards, I shall be glad to do so."

He went away, and Barry and Natalie went off by themselves, to rejoice in the fact that all veils of suspicion were lifted from them and that they had long years ahead to help one another to forget the past and make a radiant, happy future.

Joyce had a quiet knowledge that some time in the coming years she, too, would again know happiness, and all united in a sad pity for the beautiful but misguided woman whose hand wrought the tragedy of Faulkner's Folly.

THE END

Other Resurrected Press Mysteries From Carolyn Wells

Resurrected Press Mysteries From Louis Tracy

The Albert Gate Mystery
Four men murdered and a fortune in diamonds belonging to the Turkish Sultan stolen, while the Foreign Office official in charge has gone missing. Was it a common jewelry theft or was it a case of international intrigue? This is the question that barrister detective Reginald Brett must solve.

The Bartlett Mystery
When Ronald Tower is murdered on his way to a bridge game on the yacht Sans Souci it at first appears a common crime. But as Rex Carshaw finds, a tragic case of mistaken identity leads to political scandal among the rich and powerful of New York.

The Strange Case of Mortimer Fenley
When the wealthy Mortimer Fenley is struck down by a shot from an express rifle on the steps of his mansion, detectives Winter and Furneaux of Scotland Yard must find the culprit. Was it the artist who claimed he was painting a picture at the time of the shot? The disaffected younger son? Or is there another suspect?

The Stowmarket Mystery
For five generations the Fergus-Hume family has been cursed. Each of the baronets has met a violent end. When the fifth baronet is found slain by a ceremonial Japanese dagger, suspicion falls on his cousin David. It falls to barrister detective Reginald Brett to prove his innocence and find the real murder in a case that spans two continents and as many centuries.

Resurrected Press Mysteries by J. S. Fletcher

The Orange-Yellow Diamond
When an elderly pawnbroker is murdered in the London parish of Paddington, a young, down on his luck writer is accused of the crime. But then it's found the pawnbroker had had in his possession an extraordinary South African diamond worth over eighty-thousand pounds — a diamond that's now missing. It falls to Melky Rubenstein to unravel the mystery and prove the young man's innocence.

The Middle Temple Murder
When an elderly man's body is found on the steps of chambers in the Midde Temple, one of the Inns of Court, it falls to newspaperman Frank Spargo and Detective-Sergeant Rathbury to solve the crime. The murdered man, for indeed it was murder, was found with no money or identification on his person except for a piece of paper with the name and address of a young barrister. Who is the victim? Why was he killed? Who is the murderer?

Scarhaven Keep
Bassett Oliver, the famed actor, has gone missing. When Oliver fails to show for a rehearsal, aspiring playwright Richard Copplestone finds himself sent to the small village of Scarhaven on the northern coast of England to track down the actors movements. What he finds is mystery. Find the answers as Copplestone unravels the mystery of Scarhaven Keep.

Visit www.resurrectedpress.com

Resurrected Press Mysteries by Fergus Hume

The Green Mummy

Professor Braddock hoped to compare the burial practices of the Egyptians with those of the ancient Peruvians with his latest acquisition, the mummy of the last Inca, Caxas. But on arrival, the packing case proved to hold not the mummy, but the body of his assistant Sidney Bolton. It falls to Archie Hope to discover the murderer if he is to marry the professors step-daughter, Lucy Kendal. Who killed Bolton and where is the mummy? Was it the sea captain Hervey? The mysterious Don Pedro? Cockatoo the Polynesian servant? The professor, himself? And what has become of the emeralds? These are the questions that Hope must answer amongst the secrets of the past in The Green Mummy.

The Mystery of a Hansom Cab

"Truth is said to be stranger than fiction, and certainly the extraordinary murder which took place in Melbourne Friday morning goes a long way towards verifying that saying." Thus opens The Mystery of a Hansom Cab, the best selling mystery of the nineteenth century. When a man is found dead in a hansom cab one of Melbourne's leading citizens is accused of the murder. He pleads his innocence, yet refuses to give an alibi. It falls to a determined lawyer and an intrepid detective to find the truth, revealing long kept secrets along the way. Fergus Hume's first and perhaps most famous mystery... The Mystery Of A Hansom Cab.

Visit www.resurrectedpress.com

Resurrected Press Mysteries from the Dr. John Thorndyke Series

Dr. John Thorndyke - Lecturer on Medical Jurisprudence and Forensic Medicine. Before Bones, before CSI, before Quincy, M.E– there was Dr. John Thorndyke solving the most baffling cases of Edwardian London using the latest tools of medical science. Read about his cases in:

The Eye of Osiris
John Bellingham, noted Egyptologist has vanished not once but twice in the same day. Now Dr, Thorndyke must unravel the tangled claims on his estate, solve the riddle of the missing man and find the "Eye of Osiris".

The Mystery of 31 New Inn
When Dr. Jervis is whisked away in a coach with no windows to an unknown location to treat a man in a coma from undivulged causes it is Dr. Thorndyke who must come up with the solution.

The Red Thumb Mark
The first of Dr. Thorndyke's cases finds him trying to prove the innocence of a young man accused of being a diamond thief despite the fact that his finger print was found at the scene of the crime.

John Thorndyke's Cases
More cases of medical mysteries as told by his trusted assistant Jervis, M.D. Eight stories of crime and deduction in Edwardian London.

Visit www.resurrectedpress.com

Resurrected Press Mysteries by John R. Watson & Arthur J. Rees

The Hampstead Mystery

High Court Justice Sir Horace Fewbanks found shot dead in his Hampstead home, a butler with a criminal past, a scorned lover and a hint of scandal. These are the elements of the Hampstead Mystery that Detective Inspector Chippenfield of Scotland Yard must unravel with the assistance of the ambitious Detective Rolfe. But will he be able to sort out the tangled threads of this case and arrest the culprit before he is upstaged by the celebrated gentleman detective Crewe. Follow the details of this amazing case at it plays out across Hampstead, London and Scotland until it reaches a stunning conclusion in the courts of the Old Bailey.

The Mystery of the Downs

When Harry Marsland was caught in a sudden down pour he sought shelter at Cliff Farm. Met at the door by a young woman clearly expecting someone else he is only too glad to get inside to wait out the storm. When they hear a noise upstairs in the deserted house they investigate only to discover the body of the farm's owner, Frank Lumsden, dead of a gunshot wound. Who then, killed Lumsden, and why? Who was the woman expecting and did she have any roll in the murder? These are the questions that private detective Crewe must answer in The Mystery of the Downs.

Visit www.resurrectedpress.com

Other Resurrected Press Mysteries

Mysteries on a Train

Before the Orient Express there was:

The Rome Express by Arthur Griffiths
A man is found dead in his first class sleeping compartment on the express from Rome to Paris. Who was his murderer? The Countess? The English General? His brother the clergy man? The maid who has disappeared? Is the French justice system up to solving the crime? Read about it in The Rome Express.

The Passenger from Calais by Arthur Griffiths
Colonel Basil Annesley finds he is the only passenger on the train from Calais to Lucerne. That is until a mysterious woman shows up at the last minute to book a compartment. Who is after her? What is her secret? Is she a criminal or a victim? Read about it in The Passenger from Calais

Visit us at www.resurrectedpress.com

About Resurrected Press

A division of Intrepid Ink, LLC, Resurrected Press is dedicated to bringing high quality, vintage books back into publication. See our entire catalogue and find out more at www.ResurrectedPress.com.

About Intrepid Ink, LLC

Intrepid Ink, LLC provides full publishing services to authors of fiction and non-fiction books, eBooks and websites. From editing to formatting, from publishing to marketing, Intrepid Ink gets your creative works into the hands of the people who want to read them. Find out more at www.IntrepidInk.com.

www.ingramcontent.com/pod-product-compliance
Lightning Source LLC
Chambersburg PA
CBHW060921180626
46817CB00004B/1334